DEATH RIDES THE TUBE . . .

The speaking-tube whistled. Monica flew at it. "Who are you? What do you want?"

She bent her cheek to the mouth of the tube to listen for an answer. Something was happening inside the tube. She jumped back.

Something which looked like water, but was not water, spurted in a jet from the mouth of the tube. It splashed across the linoleum.

There was a hissing, sizzling noise as half a pint of vitriol began to eat into the surface of the floor.

The footsteps in the room above began to run.

A SIR HENRY MERRIVALE MYSTERY BY

CARTER DICKSON

AND SO TO MURDER

ZEBRA BOOKS
KENSINGTON PUBLISHING CORP.

ZEBRA BOOKS

are published by

Kensington Publishing Corp.
475 Park Avenue South
New York, NY 10016

First Zebra Books printing: December, 1988

Printed in the United States of America

I

In spite of herself she was excited. She had resolved that she would not allow this to show. She had pictured herself as being poised, airy, and at ease, unimpressed by the studios of Albion Films. But, now that she was actually in the office of the producer, Monica found her heart thumping and her speech a trifle slurred.

It annoyed her.

Not that there was anything about Mr. Thomas Hackett, who was to produce *Desire,* to alarm her. On the contrary. From all she had heard and read, Monica had expected to find the film studio a kind of Bedlam, full of fat men with cigars shouting lunatic orders into telephones. Not that she had actually expected to find Mr. Hackett sticking straws in his hair. But, at the same time, she was surprised and put a little off balance by the man who faced her from the other side of the desk.

The whole place — grounds, buildings, offices — struck her as being too quiet. Pineham Studios, some three-quarters of an hour by train from London, spread over many green acres behind a tall wire fence fronting the road. The main buildings, long and low like a pavilion, of dazzling white concrete with little orange awnings at the windows, were backed by the great gray shapes of the sound stages. The very sight of them brought a lump of excitement to Monica's throat. But they seemed deserted, dozing under the blaze of the late August sunlight; a little sinister.

Of course, she was not taken to the main building. The gatekeeper made this clear when her car—which she had hired at the station—pulled up before his lodge.

"Mr. H-Hackett!" Monica shouted from the back of the car.

"Who's that?"

"Mr. H-Hackett!"

"Mr. *Tom* Hackett?" inquired the gatekeeper craftily; though there was, in fact, only one Hackett at Pineham.

"That's r-right. My name is Monica Stanton. I have an appointment."

The gatekeeper took pity on her. "Old Building," he told the driver, who seemed to understand.

It was intolerably hot. The green lawns, the gravel drive, the cars parked in the drive, all winked with highlights under the sun. They drove along a gravel road past the main buildings, down a hill beneath thick-arched trees, and emerged (surprisingly) beside what resembled a small, picturesque red brick manor house with a cupola. Ivy climbed the face of the house. A miniature river, with ducks, flowed shallow and glittering in a little valley near the windows. It was idyllic. It was Arcadian. It made you want to go

6

to sleep. And upstairs, in a sunny office overlooking the stream, Monica was taken to Mr. Thomas Hackett.

Mr. Hackett was quiet, curt, and masterful—like the hero in *Desire*.

"We're happy to have you here, Miss Stanton," he said. "Happy. Please sit down."

He nodded toward a chair. With a curt, masterful gesture he yanked a box of cigars out of his desk, and thrust it at her. Then, becoming sensible of the impropriety, he returned the box to the desk and slammed the drawer with the same businesslike air.

"But you'll have a cigarette? Good! I never touch tobacco myself," he explained, with an air of virtuous austerity. "Miss Owlsey! Cigarettes, please."

He plumped down in his chair and eyed her keenly. Mr. Hackett (a personality) worked for a mysterious personage named Marshlake, the head of Albion Films, who put up the money but whom nobody ever saw except dodging round corners. Mr. Hackett bristled with practicality. His age was an alert thirty-five. He was short, stocky, and dark of complexion, with a broad face, a toothbrush mustache, and a radiant dental smile which nevertheless had an austere nononsense touch about it.

"Of course," said Monica, determined to be fair, "I'm terribly happy to be here—to have this opportunity—"

Mr. Hackett's tolerant smile acknowledged the justice of this.

"—and yet I don't want to be here under false pretenses. My agent told you, didn't he, that I've never had any experience writing film scripts?"

Mr. Hackett seemed startled. His eyes narrowed.

"No experience?" he demanded. "You're sure of that?" Mr. Hackett appeared unwilling to fall into any such trap as believing this.

"Of course I'm sure!"

"Ah, I didn't know that," murmured the producer in a soft, sinister voice; and Monica's heart sank.

Mr. Hackett considered. Then he jumped up, and strode with curt steps up and down the office. He seemed sunk in brooding thoughts.

"That's bad. That's very bad. That's not so good. — I'm just thinking aloud, you understand," he explained, suddenly looking at her and then relapsing into the same trance. "On the other hand, we don't ask you to produce a shooting script. Howard Fisk, who will direct *Desire,* never uses a shooting script. I'm telling you. Never!"

(Monica conquered an impulse to say that it was very clever of him. But, having no idea of what a shooting script might be, she remained discreetly silent.)

"Can you write dialogue?" demanded Mr. Hackett, stopping abruptly.

"Oh, yes! I wrote a play once."

"This is different," said Mr. Hackett.

"How?"

"Very different," said Mr. Hackett, shaking his head mysteriously. "But the point is — now listen to this — you can write dialogue. Good, bright, snappy dialogue?"

"I don't know. I'll try."

"Then you're hired," said Mr. Hackett handsomely. "Not too much dialogue, mind," he warned. "Keep it visual. Keep it to the minimum. In fact"—he thrust out his hands, defining the situation—"practically no dialogue at all. But you'll learn—I'm just thinking aloud, you understand. Miss Stanton, I make my decisions and I stick to 'em. You're hired."

Since Monica had already been hired, after a bitter battle on the part of her literary agent, this decision may sound superfluous. But it was not. In the film business, all things are with Allah.

For her part, Monica was so happy that she almost stuttered. It was a delirious kind of happiness, which sang in her veins and made her feel slightly drunk. She wanted to get up and say to a mirror: I, Monica Stanton, of St. Jude's Vicarage, East Roystead, Herts., am actually sitting in the offices of Albion Films, talking to the producer who made *Dark Sunshine* and *My Lady's Divorce*. I, Monica Stanton, who have so often sat in the picture-palace and seen other people's names glorified, am now to see my own name among the credit titles and my own characters come to life on the screen. I, Monica Stanton, am to be part of this vast, dazzling world—

And here it was.

2

Now Mr. Thomas Hackett, for reasons that will be indicated, was the most worried man on the Pineham lot. But, even so, he was astounded to meet Monica Stanton in the flesh. For he had gone so far as to read *Desire;* and he wondered, privately, how most of

9

it had got past the censor.

It was not that he expected Monica to resemble the voluptuous and world-weary Eve D'Aubray, the heroine of *Desire*. Just the opposite. In Mr. Hackett's experience, the ladies who wrote passionate love-stories were usually either tense business women or acidulated spinsters who petrified every male in the vicinity. He was prepared for any sort of Gorgon. What he was not prepared for was the eager, well-rounded, modest-looking girl who sat opposite him and regarded him with intelligent but innocent eyes. Without being a striking beauty, Monica was nevertheless one of those pretty, hearty, fresh-complexioned girls who radiate innocence.

In the depths of his soul, Mr. Hackett was perhaps a little shocked. He felt that she hadn't ought to know about that kind of thing. He wondered that her mother had allowed her to write the damned book.

Monica's mother was not living. But she had an aunt—and the aunt wondered too.

Everybody now knows the history of that best-selling novel, *Desire*. Everybody knows that it was written by Monica Stanton, aged twenty-two, only child of the Rev. Canon Stanton, a country clergyman; and that Monica had seldom in her life been allowed to venture beyond the confines of East Roystead, Herts. What everybody does not know is the uproar it caused in her own home.

When the manuscript was first submitted, a certain publisher said:

"Champagne by the bucket. Diamonds by the hatful. Nobody goes about in anything less than a Rolls-Royce. And love-affairs—suffering Moses! This

Captain Royce, the hero, is a devil of a fellow; though I think the author should be cautioned about letting him go tiger-shooting in Africa. But—"

"But?" asked his partner.

"In the first place, the girl can write. She'll get over this. In the second place, we don't want her to get over it. This book is a winner. It's everybody's' day-dream. The lending libraries will yell for it, or I never hope to back another."

He was right.

Monica had written it, passionately, out of every day-dream she had ever dreamed. It was not that she disliked East Roystead or even the million small duties of a parson's daughter. But sometimes she was bored to literal tears by them. Sometimes she looked at her life, lifted her fists impotently, and cried, "Grr!" This feeling was not sweetened by the presence of her aunt, Miss Flossie Stanton, one of those jolly, "sensible" women who cause more mutinies than any tyrant. So, under the lamp, Monica's imagination bloomed. In Eve D'Aubray, the heroine, she created a *grande amoureuse* whose prowess would have been looked on with respect by a combination of Cleopatra, Helen of Troy, and Lucrezia Borgia.

Monica (let this be understood) tried to keep the thing a secret. The book was ultimately published under a pen name. Nobody at home would even have known she was driving away at the story, if her aunt, in the usual course of turning over all Monica's belongings once every fortnight or so, had not come across a sheaf of manuscript in the dressing-table drawer.

Even then the family remained serene, because nobody bothered to find out what it was all about. Monica, between hot humiliation and defiant pride, announced that she was writing a book. The announcement fell flat. Her aunt smiled vaguely and said, "Are you, my dear?"— immediately changing the subject, in a somewhat pained way, to inquire whether Monica had found time in the midst of her tremendous literary labors to give the day's order to the greengrocer.

The first stir of the thunderbolt occurred with the delivery of a letter of acceptance and a real check from the publishers. The breakfast table at St. Jude's vicarage sat as though stunned. That good man, Canon Stanton, remained with the coffee-pot poised in the air for so long that the maid could stand the sight no longer, and came in and took it out of his hand. Miss Flossie Stanton went through a variety of emotions. But the check convinced her.

Whereupon Miss Stanton promptly put on her hat and went round the neighborhood to brag about it.

It was Miss Flossie's own fault. She was very casual, but she swanked like billy-o. She crammed it down people's throats. It did not occur to her to wonder what the book might be about. Originally "Monica's-little-book; so-clever-you-know" bore the noncommittal and genteel title of *Eve D'Aubray,* which Miss Stanton vaguely associated with Mrs. Gaskell and thought rather nice. Even when the book was in print, six months later, it still did not occur to her to read it.

But the tea-tables of East Roystead had read it. They were waiting. It was on Black Friday, a day in July, when Miss Stanton at the tea-table of Mrs.

12

Colonel Granby ventured the remark that she had heard it was such a nice story and wondered what it might be about. And the tea-table—trembling with secret joy—arose as one woman and told her.

That was the end.

Miss Stanton returned to the vicarage, burst into her brother's study like a dying tornado, and collapsed on the sofa. Canon Stanton resignedly put down his pen.

"James," said Miss Stanton, in a voice like a G-Man questioning a gangster under powerful lights, *"have you read that book?"*

Families have painfully literal minds.

3

And so Monica Stanton acquired the reputation of being an abandoned woman.

This is not to say that her reputation became entirely on a par with that of Eve D'Aubray in the book. After all, the people of East Roystead had known her all her life, and were quite well aware that her scope (for one thing) was more limited than Eve D'Aubray's. It was not alleged that she had first sold her honor for a diamond necklace worth twenty thousand pounds, because nobody in East Roystead ever had a diamond necklace worth twenty thousand pounds. It was not alleged that she had gone cruising in the Mediterranean with an Italian count, because everybody knew that the Stantons spent their holidays at Bournemouth.

East Roystead felt that they had to be fair.

But there it stopped. Even those who conceded that the whole thing was chiefly imagination still argued — with touching faith in the sincerity of authors — that nobody could write a whole book on one subject without having *some* knowledge of it.

Furthermore, Monica was known as a "quiet one"; and this made it worse.

The first few weeks at the vicarage were chaotic. Miss Stanton's anguished plaint was divided into three counts: (a) how they should survive the disgrace; (b) how a niece of hers could ever write of such things; and (c) how a niece of hers had ever learned of such things in order to write about them.

This last count appeared to be the most important. Miss Stanton dwelt on it to an almost gruesome extent.

Not that she ever had it out with Monica. She would demand details; and then, flushing, would lift her hand and refuse to hear them. When Monica, desperate, would demand to know exactly what she was talking about, Miss Stanton would reply, with powerful and sinister inflection, *"You* know," — and hurry in to have it out with the Canon instead.

Miss Stanton wanted to know who the man was. She reviewed, libelously, the names of all the young men in the neighborhood. In fine, she nearly drove the Canon mad; and in him Monica found an unexpected ally.

Miss Stanton regarded him with dismay.

"James, I cannot understand you. Good heavens, you cannot mean to say that you actually condone these horrible goings-on?"

14

"What goings-on?" said the Canon.

"This book, of course."

"A book, my dear, cannot properly be described as a goings-on."

"James, you are the most infuriating man I have ever known. You know quite well what I mean. This awful book—"

"It is a trifle immature, let us admit. And perhaps a little ill-advised. At the same time, I must confess that I found it mildly entertaining—"

"James, don't be revolting!"

"My dear Flossie," said the Canon, with a slight asperity, "I am tempted to be vulgar and say: Come off it. You appear to be confusing fiction with autobiography. Recently we both made the acquaintance of Mr. William Cartwright, who writes the detective novels. He made quite a favorable impression on you, if I remember correctly. You do not seriously suggest that Mr. Cartwright spends his spare time in cutting people's throats?"

Miss Stanton clutched at a tragic straw. All her troubles seemed centered on this.

"If only," she wailed, "if only Monica had written a nice detective story!"

This deserves to be included under the head of historic remarks which start family rows.

Anyone who has had some experience with family-life will testify that when the female head of a household gets hold of a remark or a piece of repartée which seems to her a good thing, she freezes to it. She never lets go. The members of her family are treated to it, in exactly the same words, on an average of a dozen times a day. Gradually it saps their vitality. They grow morbid under it. They brace themselves for its coming, each time they see the lady open her mouth.

Now Monica Stanton, to begin with, had no real grievance against the inoffensive form of entertainment known as the detective story. She neither liked nor disliked it. She had read a few, which struck her as being rather far-fetched and slightly silly, though doubtless tolerable enough if you liked that sort of thing.

But, by the time her aunt had finished, Monica was in such a state that she had come to curse the day Sir Arthur Conan Doyle was born. It was a wordless, mindless passion of hatred. As for Mr. William Cartwright—whose name Miss Flossie Stanton, with fiendish ingenuity, managed to drag into the conversation on every subject from tapioca pudding to Adolf Hitler—Monica felt that she would like to poison Mr. Cartwright with curare, and dance on his grave.

As usual, a trifle did it.

Throughout the turmoil over *Desire,* Monica had kept up a stern outer front, though she was quaking with fear inside. She had had qualms long before the storm broke. The first qualm occurred when the original hot flush of literary inspiration had passed, and she realized what she had written. The second qualm occurred when she read the proof-sheets, and writhed. Afterwards it was mostly qualms.

But she was not so much apprehensive as bewildered and furious. It wasn't fair, she cried out to the mirror. It wasn't just. It wasn't reasonable.

She had always wanted to write, and now she had

proved she could write. And what happened? What happened? She had done an admirable thing, for which she could have expected a word of praise; and instead she was treated like a convicted felon. There returned to her some of the irrational, baffled feeling of childhood, when you do something from the very best of motives, and yet instantly every adult rises against you in wrath.

"And I said to her father," declared Miss Stanton, in a heart-broken undertone, "if only Monica had written a nice detective story!"

After all, what on earth was all the fuss about? That was what Monica passionately demanded to know. Rereading *Desire* in the grisliness of cold print, she could see that there were certain passages which might be called outspoken. But what of it? What was there to be shocked about? It was perfectly normal and natural and human, wasn't it?

"And as I said to her father," confided Miss Stanton, bending closer, "if *only* Monica had written a nice detective story!"

Oh, God.

And all the worse because the book boomed into success. Tipped off by the neighbors, a newspaperman came to interview Monica. She was photographed in the vicarage garden, and her real name appeared in print. The reporter also asked her some questions about Woman's Right to Love. Monica, confused, gave some answers which sounded worse in print then they actually were. Canon Stanton had to write to his Bishop about this; Miss Stanton was furnished with spiritual ammunition for the next three weeks; and more reporters hurried to get their share of a good thing.

"You wouldn't believe it," said the *Planet,* who was himself a somewhat flighty literary turn. "Face like a Burne-Jones angel and probably a heart like Messalina."

"I dunno the dames," said the *News-Record* keenly, "but it sounds hot. Did you try to date her up?"

"Of course," observed Miss Flossie Stanton — and for the first time a hideous note of complacency began to creep into her voice — "of course, the book *is* making money; oh, yes, quite a lot, I believe; but, as I said to my brother, what is that? What is it, indeed? After all, I believe Mr. Cartwright makes quite a lot of money. And, as I said to my brother, if only Monica had written a nice *detective —* "

For Monica, that finished things.

Toward the middle of August, before there had come any glimmer of events that were to shatter Europe by the end of the month, Monica packed her bag and went to London.

4

Sitting now in the office of Mr Thomas Hackett, Monica was in almost a fever of impatience to begin work. And she would do something good, she swore to herself; she would make the script of *Desire* a screen masterpiece. For she was being treated with consideration, with courtesy, even with deference, by the man who had been described as the Young Napoleon of the British film industry. In pure gratitude for this, her loyalty went out to Mr. Hackett's curt practicality, his smooth, sure good-sense.

"Then that's settled," said Mr. Hackett, leaning across the desk to shake hands with her. "And now that you're one of us, Miss Stanton, what do you think of it?"

"I think it's wonderful," answered Monica, with sincerity. "But—"

"Yes?"

"Well, I mean—how do I work? That is, do I stay in town and write the script and send it to you? Or do I work here?"

"Oh, you'll work here," said Mr. Hackett; and Monica's joy bubbled clear to the top. It had been her one remaining anxiety. The mere sight of Pineham Studios had put the film-germ into her blood.

"It'd hardly do to have you in town," the producer went on dryly. "I've got to have you under my eye. And I've got a fellow here who can teach you the hang of the game in no time. We'll put you in the room next to him." He made a note. "But it means work, you know! Good, hard, solid work. And quick work, too, Miss Stanton. I'm keen about this. I want to go into production"—his hand hovered over the desk, and descended on it with a flat, businesslike smack—"just as soon as possible. Four weeks, if we can. Three weeks, maybe. What do you say?"

Monica was not yet used to film tactics. She took him at his word, and was staggered.

"Three weeks! But—"

Mr. Hackett considered, and made a grudging concession.

"Well, perhaps a bit longer. Not much longer,

though, mind! That's the way we work here, Miss Stanton. I want this production to follow *Spies at Sea,* our present anti-Nazi espionage film."

"I know, Mr. Hackett, but—"

"Spies at Sea should be finished by that time. I hope." A shade of hideous gloom went across his face. But he cheered up a moment later. "Say four to five weeks," he urged persuasively, "and give ourselves plenty of time. That's it. That's settled, then." He made another note. "What do you say?"

Monica smiled.

"I'll try, Mr. Hackett. All the same, please! Whether I can learn all I've got to learn, and still do you anything like a decent script for *Desire,* all in four weeks—"

Mr. Hackett regarded her rather blankly.

"For *Desire?*" he repeated.

"Yes, of course."

"But, my dear young lady," said Mr. Hackett, bustling out at her with a bland, paternal air, "you're not going to work on the script of *Desire."*

Monica stared at him.

"Oh, no, no, no, no!" continued Mr. Hackett, as though wondering what could have put such an idea into her head. He was almost reproachful about it. His dental smile flashed. He shook his head. All the force and radiance of his personality, which seemed to animate even his toothbrush mustache, was directed toward disabusing her mind of this fantastic notion.

"But I thought—I understood—"

"No, no, no, no, no," said Mr. Hackett. "Mr. William Cartwright is to work on *Desire,* and

20

he'll teach you what you need to know about the business. You, Miss Stanton, are to do us the screenplay for Mr. Cartwright's new detective novel, *And So to Murder*."

II

If Mr. Dunne's theory is correct, some very peculiar things go on in the subconscious mind. Monica, even though for a moment she was breathless with shock, had nevertheless the feeling of being able to say, "I have been here before." The whole scene — the white-painted office, the chintz curtains at sunny windows, Mr. Hackett's voice mouthing and echoing — all returned to her with horrible familiarity, as though she had been through the same scene somewhere before, and should have known what was coming.

The real reason was that, secretly, she had feared it couldn't last. It was much too good to be true. Somewhere, ran her secret conviction, the fates must be waiting to spoil her dreams again with some poisonously dirty trick.

And, when it occurred, this dirty trick would of course concern the name of Cartwright. It was inevitable. She was haunted by Cartwright. Her universe was blackened by Cartwright. At the end of every pleasant avenue, up there popped Cartwright's detestable face.

Yet she fought against it.

"You don't mean that," she pleaded, hoping against hope. "Mr. Hackett, you can't mean it!"

"I do mean it, though," said Mr. Hackett affably.

"I am to work on a detective story instead of my own book?"

"That's it exactly."

"And Mr. Cartwright" — she managed to pronounce the name, though with incredible loathing — "is to work on the script of my book, *my* book?"

"You've guessed it," beamed the producer.

"But why?"

"I beg your pardon?"

Monica was so much in awe of him that, ordinarily, she would not have had the courage to protest. She would have suffered in silence, thinking that it must somehow be her own fault. But this was too much. There rose to her lips, spontaneously, the words, "It's the silliest thing I ever heard of!" Though she did not speak these words, something of their spirit must have got into her tone.

"I said why?" she insisted. "I mean, why should we have to do each other's books instead of doing our own?"

"You don't understand these things, Miss Stanton."

"I know that, Mr. Hackett; but — "

"Miss Stanton, are you a producer of ten years' experience, or am I?"

"You are, of course; but — "

"Then that's all right," said Mr. Hackett more

cheerfully. "You mustn't try to change us all at once, Miss Stanton. Ha ha ha. We have our little ways, you know. You must just take my word for it that we know a little something about this business, after ten years' experience. Eh? And you'll learn. Yes, indeed. Why, with Bill Cartwright to teach you, you'll pick up the business in no time."

The full enormity of the proposition was gradually seeping into Monica's mind. She jumped to her feet.

"You mean," she said, "that I'm to stay here and be taught — *taught* — how to write screen plays by that — that repulsive — that *foul* — "

Her companion was interested.

"Ah? Do you know Bill Cartwright?"

"No, I don't know him. But my family have met him. And they say," cried Monica, departing from the strict letter of the truth, "they say he's the most repulsive, disgusting, funny-looking object that ever walked the face of the earth!"

"Oh, here! No, no, no."

"Indeed?"

"You've got it all wrong, Miss Stanton," the producer assured her. "I've known Bill for years. He'd never take any beauty prizes, Lord knows. But he's not as bad as all that." Mr. Hackett reflected. "In fact, I'd say he was rather distinguished-looking."

Monica choked.

To Mr. Hackett it seemed, dimly, that the little lady was annoyed about something.

For Monica had long ago built up a mental picture of Mr. William Cartwright which she refused to alter by one line. Mr. Cartwright was everywhere praised, at least in the book reviews, for the "flawless soundness and painstaking accuracy" of his plots. This made the man even more insufferable. Monica felt that she could have despised him less if only he had been a little more slipshod. She pictured him as studious-looking, withered, dry, and donnish, with enormous spectacles. And she dwelt with loving hatred on the image.

"I can't do it," she said abruptly. "I'm terribly sorry. You know how grateful I am. But I can't. It would be impossible."

"Oh, of course," said the producer, with cold indifference, "if you want to break your contract—"

"It isn't that," said Monica desperately. "Please understand me, Mr. Hackett. I'm not trying to dictate to you. I'm sure you know best." (She believed this; it was all Cartwright's fault.) "I could do anything you asked me, if only you'd tell me: *why?* Why do I have to work on a detective story, which I don't know anything about, instead of my own book, that I know every line of? Can't you please just tell me the reason?"

Mr. Hackett showed a face radiant with relief.

"Oh, the reason?" He accented the last word. "Is that all? Why didn't you say so in the first place? The reason?"

"Yes!"

"Why, my dear young lady," explained her companion, in a pitying tone, "there's nothing simpler. The reason—"

The telephone on his desk rang.

Mr. Hackett, shivering like a dynamo, seized the telephone. Everything else was instantly dismissed from his mind.

"Yes . . . yes, Kurt? . . . Yes? . . . Well, ask Howard! . . . No, no, not for a minute. The new writer has just arrived." He flashed his dental smile, a conspiratorial smile, at Monica over the top of the telephone. "Yes, very pleasant girl. . . . Yes. . . . All right, all right, I'll be there." He whipped up a pencil and made a note. "Stage three in five minutes. . . . Yes. . . . All right. . . . 'Bye."

He replaced the receiver.

"And now, Miss Stanton! What were we talking about?"

"I don't want to detain you—"

"It's all right," said Mr. Hackett, waving his hand in a way which implied that it wasn't all right but that he would have to put up with it. "Five minutes, five minutes! No hurry! What were you going to tell me?"

"I wasn't, Mr. Hackett. You were going to tell me the reason why you want me to work on a detective story instead of my own book?"

"Ah, yes! Yes. My dear Miss Stanton, there's nothing simpler. The reason—"

The door of Mr. Hackett's office was flung violently open, and a man walked in.

He did not merely walk in: he stalked in. With him there came such a current of quiet, cold, contained rage that he might have been opening the door of a refrigerator. The atmosphere of it spread round the walls and struck against the sunshine. It was evident in every aspect of his behavior. Though he hurled the door open, he did not allow it to bang against the wall; he caught it with quiet, quivering fingers and placed it gently there. Then he walked across the room with cat-footed steps, as though anxious not to

26

explode a mine. He was a tall, youngish man who carried a book under his arm. It was only when he stood by the producer's desk, looking Mr. Hackett in the eye, that the mine did explode in one blast of anguish.

He said:

"Hell's — sweet — *bells!*" And he whacked the book down on the desk with a crash which jarred the hat off a china ink-pot shaped like a mandarin.

The book was a copy of that best-selling novel, *Desire*.

Mr. Hackett reached out and replaced the hat on the mandarin.

"Hello, Bill," he said.

"Look here," said the newcomer. "This is too much. I can't do it, Tom. By God, I won't do it."

"Sit down, Bill."

The newcomer began to edge round Mr. Hackett's desk. An outsider might have thought that his intention was to strangle Mr. Hackett; as perhaps, for a moment, it was. The newcomer's voice, normally suave, was now even more suave, though with a note of hoarseness. We have heard that same note in the voices of men who go down on their knees, carefully, to talk to golfballs.

"Listen to me," said the newcomer. "I do not, in general, object to preparing screen plays for bad books. I may point out, in extenuation, that these are the only kind of books for which anybody is ever asked to prepare screen plays. Very well!"

He lifted his hand.

"But there are limits beyond which no pander of the English language, however conscienceless, can go. I have reached my limit. This book is not only eyewash. It is the most complete, unmitigated and appalling drivel ever foisted upon an unsuspecting public by illiterate maniacs masquerading as publishers. In a word, Tom, it is *lousy*. Do I make myself clear?"

He reached down and tapped the copy of *Desire*. His fingers were twitching.

"Tut, tut," said Mr. Hackett blandly. "Let me introduce you to Miss Stanton. Mr. Cartwright, Miss Stanton."

"How-do-you-do," said Cartwright, giving Monica a quick glance over his shoulder and turning back again. "To continue, Tom. This book—"

"How do you do?" said Monica sweetly. For she was happy.

It may sound odd to say this. But, in her first look at William Cartwright, she had seen something which almost compensated her for the situation. Through her hatred struck a thrill of unholy joy like the note of a diabolical tuning fork. Monica glowed to it. She felt her resolution tighten, her courage swell back, in the conviction that the enemy had been delivered into her hands.

True, her original portrait was wrong. William Cartwright was not withered, dry, and donnish, though he had an offensive habit of a striking a pose and lecturing. Ill-advised persons might have said that he was not bad-looking: he had good shoulders, good eyes, a lean face, and close-cut brown hair. Ill-advised persons (not seeing below the surface into his guilty soul) might even have said that it was a good-natured face. Monica admitted all this, for she

28

wished to be fair. In compensation, she saw about him something so awful that it was even better; something which put him completely beyond the human pale; something which must lay him open to the mercy of her derision forever. Mentally, she jumped up and down in her chair with the joy of it.

For William Cartwright had a beard.

2

Again justice must be done. It was not a W. G. Grace beard. Nor was it one of those scraggly beards abominated by everybody. On the contrary, any male would have said that it was a pretty good hirsute effort, as beards go: trim, close-clipped like the mustache, giving its owner something of the look of a naval commander.

But most women do not see it like this. Monica, temporarily color-blind, saw its tinge as red.

"I say nothing," continued the unspeakable Cartwright, sticking out his chin with the offending beard, "of bad grammar and worse syntax. I say nothing of a prose style which would sink a battleship. I say nothing of the priggish ass of a hero, Captain Whatshisname. I say nothing, even, of the pornographic mind of the woman who wrote it—"

"Oh!" said Monica, jumping involuntarily.

"Now, Bill," urged Mr. Hackett, "you shouldn't talk like that in front of Miss Stanton. Where's your manners? *(Ss-t! Oi!)*"

"I say nothing . . . What's the matter with you?

Why the hula-hula gestures?"

("That's the girl who wrote it!")

"Eh? Who is?"

("There. Behind you.")

There was a terrible silence. For a second Mr. Cartwright did not turn round. Monica had a back view of an ancient sports coat, and gray flannels which looked as though they had not been pressed since Christmas. The shoulders of the sports coat slowly hunched up until they were almost on a level with his ears.

"Good God!" he whispered in an awed voice.

Then he risked one eye, and finally turned round and faced it.

"Look here," he blurted out, "I'm sorry!"

"Sorry? Oh, no," said Monica, pale with fury but carefully keeping her voice light, airy, and la-di-da. "Please don't apologize. It's quite all right. I don't mind in the least."

"You don't mind?"

"Oh, dear me, no," said Monica, with a shivering little laugh. "I do so like to hear unbiased outside opinions about my character."

"Look: I honestly am sorry! I hope you didn't put the wrong construction on anything I said?"

"Oh, dear me, no!" said Monica, laughing with great heartiness. " 'In a word, Tom, it is lousy.' There's not much room for a wrong construction in that, surely? The wrong construction, it appears, was in my grammar."

"I tell you, I'm sorry! How was I to know it was you sitting there? I couldn't have known it! If I had known—"

Monica smiled wickedly.

"You wouldn't have spoken so?"

"No, so help me!"

"Dear, dear, dear!" said Monica. "Do you know, Mr. Cartwright, I always rather imagined you would prefer to be a hypocrite? It is so nice to hear you admit it."

Cartwright moved back a step. His (red) beard looked dazed. A thoughtless observer, not seeing through his real vileness as Monica saw through it, might have thought he was honestly contrite.

He drew himself up to his full height, and tried again.

"Madam," he said, his voice regaining its earlier richness and suavity, "madam, in case the fact has escaped your notice, I have been attempting to apologize. I was tactless. I was ill-mannered. I mean to apologize to you if it kills me."

"For you, Mr. Cartwright, surely the most painful form of suicide?"

"Now, now, you two, no quarreling," interrupted Mr. Hackett sternly. He got to his feet, brushing at the lapels of his coat. "Sorry I've got to leave you. Got to run along now. But I'm glad you two have met. I want you to work well together."

Cartwright stiffened. He turned round very slowly to look at the producer.

"You want — ?" he repeated.

"Yes. By the way: Miss Stanton is going to do the script of your detective story. Didn't I tell you?"

"No," sid Cartwright in a slow, strange voice. "No, you didn't tell me."

"Well, you know it now. And another thing! I want

31

you to be," he smiled, "a sort of guide, counselor, and father confessor to Miss Stanton. She's never had any experience with writing scripts."

"She has never had any experience," murmured Cartwright, "with writing scripts."

"That's right. So I want you to teach her; give her a hand; show her what's what. I want you both here under my eye in the Old Building. I'm giving her Les Watson's old office, next to yours. We'll clean the place up and bring in a new typewriter, and it'll be as good as new. So you can give her the hang of it, teach her the rudiments—you know!—while you're working on the script of *Desire*."

Cartwright took a little run up and down the room.

"One, two, three, four," he counted, half-closing his eyes. "Five, six, seven, eight . . . No, you don't!"

He took a long bound in front of Mr. Hackett as the producer started for the door. Reaching the door ahead of him, Cartwright closed it, turned the key in the lock, and stood with his back to it.

"I came here," he said, "to have this out with you. And you don't leave this office until I do."

Mr. Hackett stared at him.

"What the devil's the matter with you? Are you crazy? Open that door!"

"No. You are first going to listen to a few home truths. Tom, it's no business of mine how you waste your money. But, as an old friend of yours, I want to reason with you before you go completely off your chump and start making gibbering noises at windows. Do you know what you have been doing for the past three weeks?"

"Yes."

"I doubt it. Look! Three weeks ago you started making *Spies at Sea*. You lined up Frances Fleur and Dick Conyers for the leads. You had a first-rate script, and Howard Fisk to direct. A week after they had started shooting, you decided that the script was all wrong and would have to be changed."

"Are you going to open that door?"

"No. What did you do then? Get somebody here to change it? No. You sent all the way to Hollywood — I repeat: to Hollywood — and, at an expense which makes my Scotch soul shrivel, you hired the highest-paid scenario-writer in the business to come over here. The expert hasn't arrived yet. It will be days before the expert can arrive. In the meantime, what do you do? I'll tell you. You go blithely on shooting *Spies at Sea* from the original script, every foot of which will have to be scrapped when the 'expert' gets here."

Cartwright drew a deep breath. His (leprous-red) beard was bristling.

He extended quivering hands.

"Tom, if I didn't know you so well, I should think you were trying to wreck your own business. But the real trouble is that you're script-mad. Look at the present situation. Look at Miss Um-Um and me. Just put a cold compress round your head and look at it!"

Mr. Hackett's swarthy face darkened.

"I've tried to be patient with you, Bill. Will you stop this foolishness and get out of the my?"

"No."

"You realize, don't you, that you'll never get another job here?"

"Another job here," breathed Cartwright. Two powerfully gloomy eyes were bent down on the producer. "And the man holds *that* over my head as a threat! In the future, anyone who even mentions films to me will be assaulted. I have had enough! Another job? I would rather drink a pint of castor oil neat. I would rather be compelled to reread *Desire*. But surely there must be someone who can see reason in this thing. I appeal to you, Miss Um-Um. Don't you agree with me?"

Strictly speaking, Miss Um-Um did. But this was not a time to stick to the niceties of logic.

"You are appealing to me, Mr. Cartwright?"

"I am. Abjectly."

"You want my honest opinion?"

"If you please."

"Well, in that case," said Monica, puckering up her forehead, "it all depends on how you look at it. I mean, are you a producer of ten years' experience, or aren't you? Of course, if you're so swollen with conceit that you think nobody knows anything except yourself; if every time anyone makes a suggestion to you you fly into a sulk and want to go out in the garden and eat worms . . . well, it's not much good arguing, is it?"

Cartwright stared at her long and hard. Then he did a little dance in front of the door.

Mr. Hackett threw back his head and laughed.

"Now, now, we'll forget all about it!" he soothed, clapping Cartwright on the shoulder. "I know you don't mean anything by it, old man."

"I'm sure he doesn't, Mr. Hackett."

"No. Bill tears up his contract about once a week;

but he always comes round."

"I'm sure he does."

"Well, I've got to run along now. There's some trouble on the set. It seems there was a mix-up of some sort, and somebody nearly got killed. We can't have that. Bill, I leave Miss Stanton in your charge. Probably she'd like to look over the place. You might show her round, and then bring her over to stage three."

"But, Mr. Hackett!" cried Monica, suddenly filled with alarm. "Wait! Please! Just a minute!"

"Delighted to have seen you, Miss Stanton," the producer assured her, shaking hands with her and then pushing her back into her chair. "I hope we'll have a long and pleasant association. If there's anything you want to know, ask Bill. I know you'll both have a lot to talk about. Be seeing you, Bill. Good-bye, good-bye."

The door closed behind him.

3

For a full minute after he had gone, neither of them spoke. Then William Cartwright cleared his throat.

"Madam, don't say it."

"Don't say what?"

"Don't say," explained Cartwright, "whatever it was that you were about to say. Something tells me that almost any topic of conversation introduced between us is likely to prove of a controversial nature.

35

But there's one thing I should rather like to know. Do you honestly want me to show you round the place?"

"If it would not be troubling you too much, Mr. Cartwright."

"Good! Then may I ask one further question?"

"Yes. What is it?"

"Well," said Cartwright, more confidentially, "do you really see blackbeetles crawling up my collar? Have you observed any latent signs of leprosy which a close medical examination would reveal? I do not ask out of idle curiosity. I ask because I am getting nervous. Ever since I came in here, you have been sitting and looking at me with an expression—I don't know how to describe it—a sort of concentrated sick loathing, which (to be frank about it, madam) is getting me down."

"How interesting."

"All right; isn't it true?"

"You must excuse me," said Monica, arranging her skirt over her exceedingly shapely legs with a disdain that would have done credit to Eve D'Aubray herself. "I don't care to discuss the subject any further."

"Yes, but I do. Hang it all!" shouted Cartwright, volplaning down into honest speech. "Why can't you be reasonable? I've apologized, haven't I? What else can I do?—Not that I take back any of my opinions, mind!"

Monica began to shiver.

"Really?" she said. "How extremely kind of you. How terribly, *terribly* generous of you."

"Yes. And I can quite understand how you feel. I can make every allowance for your wounded vanity—"

Monica, merely stupefied, sat back in her chair and stared at him. But she could not see him. She saw only a dim outline through a floating, luminous mist of hatred which had accumulated in her brain like smoke out of a genie-bottle. Completely unknown to herself, her skirt slipped up over her knees. She did not observe Cartwright's expression of gloomy, cynical satisfaction, which was nevertheless mixed with angry surprise.

"Every allowance," he repeated, holding up his hand pontifically, "for your wounded vanity. But (don't you see?) there's got to be such a thing as an artistic conscience."

"Indeed?"

"Yes. I am sorry to say it, but your novel is eyewash. It is the product of an immature mind exclusively concerned with one subject. Such people as your Eve D'Aubray and your Captain Whoozis do not exist and never could exist."

Monica sprang up.

"And I suppose," she blazed at him, "your silly little murders could exist?"

"My dear young lady, let us not argue about that. Such things are based on scientific principles, and are altogether different."

"They are nasty, footling little tricks that would never work in a thousand years. And they're so badly written that they make me sick."

"My dear young lady," said Cartwright, in a gentle and world-weary tone, "aren't we merely being childish now?"

Monica got a grip on herself. She was Eve D'Aubray again.

"I daresay we are. Please, before I say something I shall regret, will you be good enough to take me wherever it is you're going to take me? That is, if you really meant it."

"Are you going to tell me," said Cartwright stubbornly, "why you hate my guts?"

"Really, Mr. Cartwright!"

"Oh, come off it."

"You dare!"

"But you do hate 'em, don't you?" he demanded, thrusting out the red beard.

"Dear, dear," murmured Monica. "Don't you flatter yourself, rather? I really hadn't given it much consideration. If you ask me whether I feel a mild dislike of you and your manners and your bea—I mean, of everything about you, why, I'm afraid I must say yes."

"Well, I don't dislike you."

"I beg your pardon?"

"I said I don't dislike you," roared Cartwright.

"How interesting," said Monica.

It was unfortunate that she detested him so much. Before an hour had elapsed, in the evil forces that were gathering round Pineham Studios, she had to thank him for saving her life from the first attempt of a murderer.

III

Even before that hour had elapsed, Monica herself was beginning to regret that she detested him so much. If she had not known better, she might have been deceived into thinking him courteous and considerate. Also, he smoked a curved pipe of the Sherlock Holmes variety; an abomination.

"But why do we have to work down here?" she wanted to know. "Why aren't we up in that big building with the awnings?"

"Because," said Cartwright, "Albion Films isn't the only outfit here. There are three others. Radiant Pictures and S.A.G.—American companies—and Wonderfilms, who built the studios in the first place. They hire sound stages and offices, just as we do. These grounds were originally a private estate, and the Old Building was the manor house, before Dega of Wonderfilms bought it." An expression of dreamy and evil glee went over his face. "Radiant Pictures are doing a super-colossal spectacle based on the life of the Duke of Wellington. I've been talking to Aaronson; and if his version of the Battle of Waterloo doesn't turn out to be a joy and delight forever, it won't be my fault."

"Oh? I suppose that's your idea of being funny?" Cartwright laid hold of his hair and pulled.

"All right, all right. Sorry! Change the subject, quick!"

But Monica was bristling.

"And just a wee bit childish, don't you think? I suppose you'd do the same to Mr. Hackett, if he didn't pay you your salary. After all, what call have you to look down on Mr. Hackett?"

"I don't."

"Yes, that's obvious, isn't it? But *he* doesn't put on any side. When I came out here, I expected to have to interview at least a dozen secretaries, and maybe sit all day in an outer office without seeing him at all. But no. There he was, just as accessible and pleasant and human—"

"Well, why shouldn't he be? He's no ruddy little tin god."

"Aren't you being rather spiteful now?"

"Listen to me," said Cartwright. "One thing I should like to make clear. This is not a bad place to work. In English films, you get very little of the Hollywood high hocus-pocus and mysticism. People don't lock themselves away into secret shrines behind a battery of secretaries. And everybody knows everybody else. From producer to director to star and all the way down, they're all over the place. They drop in on each other, and hang about, and get in your way. They are mostly a very decent crowd. Some of them, even, are quite intelligent. Only—"

"What?"

"You'll see," answered Cartwright, with gloomy relish.

It is doubtful whether she heard him. They had emerged into hot sunlight beside the manor house, and were walking up a broad, smooth slope of greensward at the curve of the lake.

Parts of this lake had served, on various occasions, as the Thames, the Seine, the Euphrates, the Grand Canal, the Bosphorus, the Atlantic and/or Pacific Ocean. At the moment there was evidently a submarine in it, for Monica could see the grim deck and conning-tower. An inquisitive duck cruised round this, eyeing it. Beyond, where the lake narrowed, it was spanned by a footbridge leading to a path into some woods; and there was a large notice-board reading, "NO VISITORS PERMITTED BEYOND THIS BRIDGE." Up the hill to their right—the side permitted to visitors—were the blank backs of the sound stages, rising above trees. The middle of this parkland was ornamented by the façade of a noble Georgian manor house, white and pillared, propped up with such skill that it required a second look before you realized it was only a shell. To Monica the sight of it brought a quicker heart-beat, the hot thrill of make-believe.

And it emboldened her to ask a question.

"Mr. Hackett mentioned," she began; and stopped breathless.

"Yes?"

"He said something about an actress named Frances Fleur. Do you know her?"

"F.F.? Yes. What about her?"

"Nothing; I was only asking. What's she like? Is she nice?"

Cartwright reflected. "F.F.? Yes, I suppose so.

Quite a good scout." He paused, and regarded her narrowly above the sun-gleaming beard; it was a shrewd glance, as though pinning her to the wall. He seemed about to speak, and then changed his mind. He added, casually: "You've seen her on the screen, I suppose?"

"Once or twice."

"Like her?"

"She's very pretty," said Monica primly.

Though Monica would have died rather than admit it, the shadow-appearance of Frances Fleur on the screen had been the inspiration for the looks and mannerisms of Eve D'Aubray. There were times when Frances Fleur became Eve D'Aubray; and Monica Stanton, in imagination, became both.

"What's she like? Is she married?"

"Several times, I believe. Her first venture was with Lord Somebody-or-Other, when she was in musical comedy."

"Lord Roxbury of Brene," said Monica automatically.

"Something like that. Her second venture, more recent and still in operation, is with Kurt Gagern, or von Gagern."

Monica stared at him. "But I never heard of *him!*"

"You will," the other assured her. "Gagern is the rising star hereabouts. He was a director for UFA before the Nazis threw him out of Germany. He's strict Aryan; one of the old von-und-zu aristocrats, I believe; but he didn't get on well there. He's now assistant director to Howard Fisk for *Spies at Sea*. In some way he hypnotized the Admirality into letting him get all the authentic naval stuff, for exteriors, at

Portsmouth and even at Scapa Flow."

There was a curious tone in Cartwright's voice, which Monica did not notice. In the first place, she was rather annoyed with her idol for getting married without her knowledge. In the second place, they had now come round to the front of the main building.

Inside, where it was cool, she found the atmosphere she had been expecting: the atmosphere of hurry, ultimatums, and slammed doors. The building was a hive of long galleries, with little offices set side by side like ships' cabins; and most of the activity seemed to consist of opening and shutting doors. People stalked; typewriters ticked; there was a heavy smell of paint. A page-boy emerged from the canteen, eating a chocolate bar. Cartwright went down a long open passage—a sort of glass-enclosed Bridge of Sighs—running through bright gardens to the sound stages at the far end.

The corridor beyond was immense. It was of concrete, rapping with echoes, and reminded Monica of an airport. From it, sound-proof doors opened into the stages. The red light was burning over the door of number three, to show that you must not open the door during sound-recording. Cartwright beckoned Monica to wait; and he listened, with diabolical glee, to the conversation of two men who were standing in the middle of the corridor.

One was a short fat man with a cigar, the other a tall spectacled young man with an ultra-refined accent.

"Lookit," said the fat man. "This ballroom sequence."

"Yes, Mr. Aaronson?"

"This blowout," explained the fat man, "that the Duchess of Richmond give before the Battle of Waterloo."

"Yes, Mr. Aaronson."

"Well, I've just seen the rushes. It's lousy. There ain't enough hot-cha in it."

"But, Mr. Aaronson—"

"Now lookit," said the fat man. "What it wants, see, is a song for Erica Moody to sing. Luke Fitzdale, he's just turned out a hot number that's a honey. So here's what we do, see? The Duke of Wellington says, 'Ladies and gentlemen, we got a big surprise for you tonight,' see? So the Duchess of Richmond sits on the piano and sings it."

"But I really don't think she would have done that, Mr. Aaronson."

"You don't think so?"

"No, Mr. Aaronson."

"Well, that's what she's going to do in this picture. And another thing. There's another spot for a song that's a natural. We'll have her sing before the battle, to cheer the troops up. I got it all figured out. The Duchess of Richmond—"

The red light over the door went out.

"In you go," said Cartwright. He knocked out his curved pipe against the wall, and pushed Monica ahead of him into darkness.

2

The sound stage inside was rather like a barn, a

44

Gargantuan barn covering some half an acre. Like a barn it was darkish and cluttered. It looked a hundred feet high. Hollowly, innumerable small noises made a tinkling background: footsteps, iron cables dragging, the rasp of a saw, muttered voices. Though there appeared to be a good many persons moving about, they moved as shadows. Lights, dead-pale lights—all very distant, and none apparently directed toward what you were looking at—threw a bluish pallor to join the few gleams of daylight from under the roof.

It was a mass and a mess. They had built everybody's house, everybody's garden, everybody's nightmare; built it, and then broken it up.

With Cartwright's hand firmly clasping her elbow, Monica stumbled through a submerged world. Fragments of a prison (the black-painted wooden bars looking very unconvincing) were stacked in flats against one wall. They passed a hotel kitchen, and a part of Westminster Bridge. They crossed a suburban street, of which the principal house—that of a homicidal physician, from a story by William Cartwright—was a complete, practical-built house from the last gray-painted brick outside to the last stick of furniture inside. The street looked bluish and dingy and unpleasantly sinister. It seemed to Monica that they had been groping for miles before a murmur of voices rose ahead, and a core of brilliant light became visible across the floor.

"Silence, please!" shouted a voice. *"Silence!"*

"There she is," said Cartwright.

They were looking, as though deep under a hood, into the bedroom of a luxury suite aboard an ocean liner. And in the middle of the cabin, wearing a low-cut gold evening-gown out of which her full shoulders rose superbly, stood Frances Fleur.

The aching clarity of the light made every color and detail more vivid than life. Pink-and-white paneled walls, white upholstery, mahogany round the porthole-windows, all glowed and glistened. The toilet articles on the dressing-table appeared to be made of gold; the white door stared; even the lamp and the water-bottle glittered on the table by the bed. Frances Fleur's makeup, the skin a super flesh-tint like orange-gold, contrasted with her long, narrow eyes and rich black hair. The face was broad and rather high of cheekbone, incuriously placid, and the eyebrows looked as though they had been painted on oiled silk.

"Look out for that cable!" muttered Cartwright, and caught Monica as she tripped. She had been walking on tiptoe since their entrance. "Move over here. Ss-t!"

"Silence, pul-lease!"

All noise was blotted out. At the edge of the lights there were silhouettes, ghost-faces, and the Martian shapes of machinery.

"Roll 'em!"

A faint bell rang twice. A young man in a sweater stepped out in front of the camera, holding up a smallish square wooden board.

"Spies at Sea. Scene number thirty-six. Take two."

The lower edge of the board, set on a spring, clicked sharply. The young man stepped back. And Frances Fleur came to life.

The plump, handsome brunette seemed undecided. Her features expressed this. She moved her smooth

46

shoulders above the gold gown. She glanced toward the door. Then she pressed a bell-push. With a celerity unknown in any ocean-liner since the Ark, her summons was answered by a stewardess.

This stewardess, obviously, was up to no good. She was a middle-aged woman with a tough, leering face. Any Secret Service agent, after one glance at that dial, would promptly have locked away his papers and sat down to guard them with a gun.

"You rang, my lady?"

"Yes. Did you deliver my message to Mr. De Lacy?"

"Yes, my lady. Mr. De Lacy will be here at once."

"Cut!" whispered a new voice.

Then everything stopped.

Monica's first impression was that something must be wrong. But neither Frances Fleur nor the sinister stewardess nor anybody else seemed to find anything unusual in it. They merely waited. The sinister stewardess, it is true, appeared to be in a state of agitation bordering on tears. Otherwise everything seemed to move in slow-motion.

After a decent interval, evidently for consultation in the gloom, a tall, gray-haired, semi-bald man stepped out on the set. He was very thoughtful. He wore a modest tweed suit, a mild-colored pull-over, and huge country shoes. The lights glinted on his mild pince-nez, and the high, narrow arch of his forehead. Monica, having seen his picture, knew him at once for Howard Fisk, the director.

What Mr. Fisk said to the two actresses is not known. If he had a fault, it was that of being almost completely inaudible. At a distance of more than six feet, it was difficult for the keenest ear to detect a single word he said. To Monica—who had rather expected him to yell through a megaphone, and bring down the house—this came as a shock.

But he made gestures. He patted the sinister stewardess on the back, and seemed to be talking kindly to her. He held an intimate and ghostly conversation with Frances Fleur; interrupted by long pauses during which he looked thoughtfully round the set, and appeared to meditate. Finally, he nodded, smiled to them, waved his hand, and left the set.

Monica drew a breath of relief.

"Spies at Sea. Scene number thirty-six. Take three."

The sinister stewardess appeared again.

"You rang, my lady?"

"Yes. Did you deliver my message to Mr. De Lacy?"

"Yes, my lady. Mr. De Lacy will be here at once."

"Cut!"

Mr. Fisk walked out on the set. His visit was rather longer on this occasion.

"Spies at Sea. Scene number thirty-six. Take four."

The sinister stewardess appeared again.

"You rang, my lady?"

Monica could not control herself. "But why don't they get on with it?" she whispered. "Why do they keep taking just that little bit over and over again?"

"Sh!" hissed Cartwright.

"But how many times are they going to take it?"

This question was answered by the sinister stewardess herself. The agitation of the sinister stewardess had been steadily growing throughout. When asked for the sixth time whether she had delivered the mes-

sage to Mr. De Lacy, she lost her nerve, said, "No,"
and burst into tears.

Mr. Fisk was understood to say that they would
take a short break.

3

"Well?" inquired Cartwright. "How did you like
it?"

"It's the most fascinating thing I ever saw."

"So! — You don't by any chance notice anything
wrong here?"

"Wrong?"

Monica stared at him. The group round the set had
begun to dissolve. A sound truck clattered, setting
the lights vibrating; some of them had been turned
off. William Cartwright stood looking from side to
side, hesitantly, as though he were sniffing the pow-
der-scented air. The curved pipe, empty, was again
hooked to his lower teeth. He seemed quite serious.

"Wrong," he insisted, making the pipe waggle. "In
the first place, though I've seen several people have
hysterics with good reason, I never knew it to happen
to old MacPherson before." He nodded toward the
sinister stewardess, who was still standing on the set,
being comforted by Howard Fisk. "There's something in the air. Half the people here have the jitters;
and I wish I knew why."

"Aren't you imagining things?"

Miss Frances Fleur had walked regally off the set.
She was now sitting on a camp-stool not far away

from them, just beyond the range of the lights. She was alone except for a real maid who even here wore a cap and apron, and who was studying her make-up. It was difficult to associate Frances Fleur with any nervousness. Her placidity looked unbroken and unbreakable. During the long monologues of Howard Fisk, she had merely nodded and smiled and done it all over again. She did not appear to be thinking about anything.

"In the second place," pursued Cartwright, "it's unnatural. There are too few people here."

"You call this too few?"

"I do. To say nothing of extras, where's the usual gang of visitors, friends, retainers, and hangers-on? Look! The place is practically deserted. You and F.F. and MacPherson and F.F.'s maid are the only women here. I don't even see the continuity-girl: which is impossible. Something's wrong."

"Still—"

"Oh, it's probably nothing. But I was wondering about Tom Hackett. Anyway, there's your F.F. in the flesh. Would you like to meet her?"

"I would, rather. I'd been wondering whether I ought to or not."

"Why not?"

Monica had a burst of honesty. "I've sometimes wondered whether she might not turn out to be some dreadful pain in the neck. But she doesn't look like that."

"She isn't. . . . Frances!"

The large brunette turned her head from staring at nothing, and smiled. She seemed to come to life exactly as she had come to life before the camera.

"Frances, may I present a great admirer of yours? Miss Stanton, Miss Fleur."

"How do you do?" smiled Miss Fleur.

She was transfigured. Her smile grew warm, showing fine teeth. Yet she did not, so to speak, turn it on. The process was not as mechanical as that. Her charm of manner was perfectly genuine; she liked to be liked; and, when you expressed admiration for her, it pleased her and you felt the physical glow of response which emanated from her.

"Miss Stanton," Cartwright explained, "is here to do some work for Tom Hackett. By the way, she is the young lady who wrote *Desire*."

Frances Fleur paused in examining a scarlet fingernail, and looked up. So far she had seemed amiable but perfunctory. It was slightly different now. She looked at Monica. She looked at her again.

"Not—"

"Yes," said Cartwright firmly.

"Is it really? How nice to meet you! That's to be my next part, you know."

Monica stared at her.

"Eve," explained Miss Fleur. "Not Eve in the garden of Eden, that is, but Eve in your book. Do come and sit down here. I must talk to you. Eleanor, bring a chair for Miss Stanton."

Eleanor did so. Monica was placed in such a position that Miss Fleur could see her in a good light. For Miss Fleur was genuinely curious. She had not actually read *Desire,* but she had got her husband to read all the best bits aloud to her; and she was interested. Her appraising glance ran and rang like a cash-register. What she thought was not apparent.

"Is this your first visit here?" she asked. "I hope you like it. I did so enjoy your book." Here she looked at Monica even more curiously.

"It's awfully good of you to say so."

"Not at all," laughed the other. "My husband—Baron von Gagern—loved it too. He chooses all my parts. You must meet him. Kurt! Kurt!"

She looked round.

"Where on earth is Kurt? It's not like him to disappear like that. Have you seen him?"

"No," answered Cartwright. "And I haven't seen Tom Hackett, though he must be here somewhere."

A glance flashed between them. Frances Fleur's eyes were very expressive. "In that case," she went on, deliberately avoiding whatever subject he meant to introduce, "she must meet Howard, of all people. Howard! Will you come over here a moment, please?"

The director administered a last squeeze to the shoulder of the sinister stewardess, who was wiping her eyes. He seemed to have cheered her up considerably. Then he lumbered across in his big shoes. Seen at close range, he had the appearance of a distinguished doctor or scientist. He was rubbing his hands together, in a smiling and satisfied way, as he approached the group. At a distance of three feet his mild voice became audible.

"Well, we're getting on," Howard Fisk confided. "Yes, definitely we're getting on." He stopped to reflect. "One of those takes ought to do. And Annie MacPherson is feeling much better."

"Howard, may I introduce the new script-writer?"

Mr. Fisk woke up.

"Ah, yes. The expert from Hollywood. Hackett mentioned it. How do you do?" he said, enfolding Monica's hand in a large paw, and beaming on her. "I hope you won't find our English ways too slow for you."

"No," said Cartwright, slowly and distinctly. "This is another person. Miss Stanton wrote *Desire*. She has never had any film experience."

Mr. Fisk patted her hand.

"Is that so? Then you're still more welcome. Were you watching the takes? What did you think of them?"

"She thought you took a devil of a long time over them," answered Cartwright, with (deliberate?) tactlessness. Monica, hot and tongue-tied, could have flown at his beard and pulled it. Her anguish was the worse in that both Frances Fleur and Howard Fisk were smiling at her. And her mind seethed with the injustice of it. She was suddenly conscious of a great shrewdness behind Mr. Fisk's pince-nez.

"You mustn't confuse patience with incompetence," the director told her. "Unfortunately, the first requisite here is patience. And the second." He meditated. "And the third. Besides, we had an unpleasant bit of business at the rehearsal."

"So?" said Cartwright. "Is that why Tom Hackett told us there'd been a mix-up in which someone nearly got killed?"

Mr. Fisk was amused. He continued to pat Monica's hand: it was beginning to make her uncomfortable.

"Tut, tut! Nothing like that. Only a foolish piece of carelessness on somebody's part. I'm going to be firm with those property men this time."

"But what happened?"

A shade of discomfort passed over the director's face. Still without relinquishing Monica's hand, he turned round and nodded toward the set.

"You see that water bottle? On the table beside the bed? There — just by the door?"

"Yes."

Though less well lighted now, the rich colors of the cabin still showed like a distant picture postcard. Again they noted the glass water bottle on the table beside the bed, spick and span and glistening.

"There was no harm done, I'm glad to say. Though Annie MacPherson got a shock, because she was nearest. We were all on the set at rehearsal, and I was explaining the business to Frances and Annie. I can't think how it came to happen."

"Go on!"

"Well, I was moving about; and making gestures, I suppose. Gagern and I were talking, and I was walking backward, and he said, 'Look out!' I bumped into that little table by the bed, and over it went. There was a sizzling kind of noise, rather unpleasant. The water bottle had fallen off on the bed, fortunately. A whole section of the counterpane, and the sheets underneath, and even the mattress, started to shrivel and blister and rot away like wasp-holes in an apple. The water bottle hadn't been full of water. It was full of oil of vitriol — sulphuric acid."

IV

"Sulphuric acid?" repeated Cartwright.

He took the empty pipe out of his mouth. There was an expression on his face which Monica could not read.

"Let me get this straight," he said. "Are you under the impression that it was a mistake on the part of the prop department?"

"Of course."

"Yes. One property man says to another, 'Oi, Bert: this bottle. There's no water tap handy, so just fill her up with sulphuric acid; it's the same color.' God Almighty!"

"You don't know the facts."

"What are they, then?"

"Sh!" urged the director, trying to make his voice louder and whirring in the effort. He released Monica's hand, and addressed her with a confidential air. "That's the trouble with these writers, Miss Stanton. Particularly Cartwright here. All"—he made gestures as of a balloon rising—"up in the air. Cartwright can see an ingenious poisoning plot in green-apple colic.

Still, we must be charitable. After all, that's his business."

He looked tolerantly at the offender.

"What are you suggesting, my boy? That it was deliberate?"

"What do you think?"

Fisk's eye was quizzical. "I know, I know. You're hot on the scent of a mystery. It was all a trap. Somebody — during the course of the shooting — was to pour out a glassful of sulphuric acid, and drink it off in mistake for water. Somebody was to get it spilled over him, or thrown in his face. Was that your idea?"

Frances Fleur shivered slightly. Throughout this she had not moved; her eyes seemed to have been turned inward. She lifted her hand and passed it over her thick, glossy black hair, which was parted in the middle and trained down to heavy waves across her cheeks. Then, with her finger-tips, she lightly touched her face.

It was a suggestive movement. She shivered again. Howard Fisk laughed.

"Now listen to the facts, my boy," he said firmly. *"That water bottle didn't figure in the scene at all."*

"Meaning what?"

"Just that. Nobody was to drink a glass of water. Nobody was to pour out a glass of water. In fact, nobody was to touch the bottle or go anywhere near the table. Do you follow that?"

"H'm."

"The bottle was just a piece of property. In the ordinary course of events, it would have been removed when the set was dismantled, emptied, and

56

put away on the shelf. It was only a million-to-one chance that I, in my clumsiness—which I admit—happened to knock the whole thing over. Very well! I know you've got imagination, my lad. I admire you for that. But, tut, tut! Suppose somebody did put the stuff there maliciously? Suppose somebody did intend to do damage? What in the world would be the sense of planting a pint of sulphuric acid in the one place where it couldn't possibly hurt anybody?"

There was silence.

Howard Fisk more than ever resembled a distinguished doctor, expounding something. Little wrinkles radiated from the corners of his eyes behind the pince-nez. He kept his hand on Monica's shoulder, and his tweed coat was redolent.

"But, hang it all, what did you do?"

"Do? Why, we had the bedding changed and went on," said the director simply.

"No. What I mean is: didn't anybody show the least curiosity as to how the acid got there? Didn't you inquire into it?"

"Ah, that. Yes, I believe Gagern was trying to." He craned his neck round. "Gagern was upset about it. I don't know what he found out. And Hackett, when *he* got here, had very definite ideas about it: he's a whirlwind, that fellow is. He seems to think it must have been sabotage."

"Sabotage?"

"Yes. *Spies at Sea,*" explained the director, to Monica, "is very strongly—and, I hope, effectively—anti-Nazi. Hackett seems to think that some heiling enthusiast may have tried to put a spoke in it. Tut, tut! That's no way to go about sabotage. But as for

57

me, I don't want them to get worried. Besides, we can't have the ladies alarmed, can we?" He winked at Frances Fleur. "Slowly and easily. Gently, gently. Step by step! That's the way to do things. I think I can assure you there is absolutely no troub . . ."

A voice spoke sharply:

"Howard! Bill! Will you come over here, please?"

The voice belonged to Mr. Hackett. He was standing near the set. There was sweat on his swarthy forehead, and his wiry black hair looked rumpled.

"So!" observed Cartwright. "You may say, if you like, that a bottle of the deadliest corrosive acid known to chemistry knocking about like water is a mere entertaining blunder on the part of the prop department. Nevertheless, I will make you a small bet. I will bet you that there is real trouble now, and that Tom Hackett has found the body. Come on. — Will you excuse us for a moment? Frances, I leave Miss Stanton in your charge."

Monica watched them go. She was roused by Frances Fleur's voice.

"Don't you like Bill Cartwright, my dear?"

"I-beg-pardon?"

"Your expression. It was positively murderous," said Miss Fleur, with real interest. "Don't you like him?"

"I loathe him."

"But why?"

"Don't let's talk about him. I—I—Miss Fleur, are you *really* going to play Eve D'Aubray?"

"I expect I am, if anybody does."

"If anybody does?"

"Well, my husband says that if there's a war it will

58

be very bad for the film business. He says that Hitler has just made an alliance with the Russians, and that's very bad too. And don't mind Howard: just between ourselves, there is something very queer going on here."

"That acid, you mean?"

"That. And other things."

"But weren't you at all nervous when the acid tipped over?"

"My dear," said Miss Fleur, "when I was on the stage they shot me out of a cannon once. That is the sort of thing men expect you to do, and they get extremely annoyed if you don't, so it's best to do it. And in one of the Blenkinsop shows they made me dive thirty feet into a glass tank without any clothes on. I *did* have a headache by the end of the run. But vitriol—ugh! No!"

"You do like the part, don't you? Eve D'Aubray, I mean?"

"It's terribly good. May I have a mirror, Eleanor, please?"

"You see, I wrote it for you."

Frances Fleur paused in the act of holding up the mirror, and tilting her head back to study the dark red make-up of her mouth.

"You see, I thought it would suit you."

Miss Fleur handed the mirror back to her maid. Her eyes, of a dark amber color under waxy-looking lids and brows on which the eyebrows made thin lines, now had a curious expression.

"It is a bit like me," she conceded, after reflection. "Fancy your knowing that! And fancy your knowing . . . how old are you? Nineteen?"

"I'm twenty-two!"

The other woman lowered her voice. "Well, I'll tell you something. I—"

It was not to be heard. Frances Fleur, bending forward, happened to glance over Monica's shoulder toward the other end of the sound-stage. Her look hardly altered, nor did her voice; it slipped so smoothly into another sentence that it was as though she had been saying this all the time.

"Please don't think me rude, but I must go. There's something I must see to at once. You do understand, don't you? I have so enjoyed our talk. We must go on with it another time, and soon. There are several things I'm dying to ask you, if you know what I mean. But now—well, you do understand. Of course. Eleanor! Follow me, please."

She swept to her feet, magnificent in the gold gown, stirring the air with faint perfume as she rose. Leaving Monica with a stricken sense of having said the wrong thing somehow, Frances Fleur smiled with ineffable sweetness as though to an audience, beckoned to her maid, and swept away.

2

So she only looked nineteen years old, did she? Grr.

Pulling another chair closer with the toe of her slipper, Monica Stanton hooked her heels over the rung of the chair, planted her elbows on her knees and her chin on her fists; and brooded.

Above all things she had wanted to impress Frances Fleur as a woman of the world: a subtle, world-weary person who might have graced the marble benches of ancient Rome. She had geared herself to do this, to such an extent that she barely heard a word of what was being said around her; and instead she got nineteen years old when she was actually twenty-two and thought she looked a good twenty-eight.

All noises in the dim, echoing barn went unheeded. A property man passed in front of her, carrying a big mirror. Monica was confronted with her own image: her heels cocked up on the chair-rung, her chin in her fists, and her mouth darkly mutinous. She saw the fair hair, worn in a long bob; the wide-spaced eyes, of a shade between gray and blue; the short nose and full under-lip; the plain gray tailored suit, with white blouse: all in contrast to the broad charms of Lady Thunder. As a result of this inspection, Monica made such a hideous, bitter face at the mirror — not unmixed with the suggestion of a raspberry in pantomime — that the property man, who was looking straight into her unseeing eyes and had worked hard all day, was not unnaturally indignant.

Frances Fleur must think her an awful ass.

And yet, in a dim sort of way, it seemed to her that there was something not quite right about Frances Fleur.

She hesitated over this. It was not that she was disappointed; not *exactly*. No! Miss Fleur was undoubtedly beautiful. And she was very pleasant. Nobody could help liking her. Yet it seemed to Monica, whose mind worked even in a bedazzled haze, that she was not very intelligent.

It also seemed to Monica, who was very fond of ancient Rome, that Miss Fleur somehow did not belong there. That phrase, "My husband says—" slipped over her tongue with the glibness of long use. Monica had a very keen ear in this respect, since Miss Flossie Stanton's conversation was almost exclusively concerned with, "My brother says—" or, "As I said to my brother." Again, to be fair. It was not that she expected Miss Fleur, in private life, to sparkle with epigrams, recline among doves and courtiers, and call for the liquidation of Christians: which, as every film-goer knows, is the only thing anybody did do in ancient Rome. But there are feelings in these things. There is instinct and sure knowledge. And it occurred to her that Miss Frances Fleur had not got the right Roman spirit.

Whereas the unspeakable Cartwright, on the other hand—

"Miss!" said a voice beside her. "Miss Stanton!"

She did not hear it.

She saw a mental picture of Cartwright dressed up in a Roman toga, his Sherlock Holmes pipe in his mouth and his hand uplifted for didactic utterance. She sat back and whooped with laughter; the first time she had laughed that day.

Bad as he was, give the man his due. Cartwright as an ancient Roman would not do too badly. He would argue the ears off the *quirites* and sit up all night explaining why somebody's epic poem was rubbish. If only he would shave off that sun-glinting, that lint-catching, that super-comical beard.

A voice at her elbow urged:

62

"Please, miss!"

Monica descended from the Palatine Hill to find a page-boy, all shining face and shining buttons, plucking at her sleeve. Having caught her attention, the page threw out his chest and intoned.

"Mr. Hackett says, will you come with me, please?"

"Yes, of course. Where?"

"Mr. Hackett says," piped the boy, with the air of a miniature sergeant major, "will you go to the practical house on Eighteen-eighty-two, and see him in the back room?"

"Where?"

"It's a set, miss. I'll-show-yer."

He strode ahead, his chest out and his arms swinging. Monica looked round. She could not see Cartwright or Hackett or Fisk or anyone else she knew. The sound and camera crews were packing up and leaving; it gave Monica an odd feeling of uneasiness. She wished everyone weren't leaving.

She ran after the boy, whom she could have sworn she had seen somewhere before. But she could not place him. He led her down an aisle, between long rows of stuffy-smelling canvas flats, back in the direction toward the door of the sound stage. It was dark except for an illuminated clock on the wall, the hands indicating a few minutes past five. Two men stood under it.

Dimly, the clock illuminated the heads of two men. One was a short fat man with a cigar, the other a tall spectacled young man with an ultra-refined accent.

Monica heard their voices as she passed.

"Lookit," said the fat man. "This battle sequence

we're going to shoot."

"Yes, Mr. Aaronson?"

"It's lousy. There ain't enough feminine interest in it. Here's what I want you should do. I want you should have the Duchess of Richmond in the battle, right alongside of the Duke of Wellington."

"But the Duchess of Richmond wouldn't be on the field-marshal's staff, Mr. Aaronson."

"Jeez, don't I know that? We got to make it sound probable or the public won't fall for it. So here's what we do. The other officers are all drunk, see?"

"Who are, Mr. Aaronson?"

"The Duke of Wellington's staff. They been out on a party with a lot of French dames, see—get some shots of that—and they're all drunk as hoot-owls."

"But, Mr. Aaronson—"

"Well, the Duchess of Richmond comes in and finds 'em lying all over the floor, see? Just so pickled they can't even move. And she's scared, because one of 'em is her brother, see, who's an officer in the Bengal Lancers. Catch on? She's afraid the Duke of Wellington may get sore if he finds out her brother's got a snootful on the morning of the Battle of Waterloo. That's all right, ain't it? He would have put up a beef about it, wouldn't he?"

"Yes, Mr. Aaronson."

"Sure. And the Duchess of Richmond, see, has got to save the family honor. So she puts on her brother's uniform and gets up on his horse and there's a lot of smoke and nobody notices the difference. How's that? Boy, is that idea a lallapalooza or ain't it?"

"No, Mr. Aaronson."

"You don't like it?"

"No, Mr. Aaronson."

"You think it stinks?"

"Yes, Mr. Aaronson."

"Well, that's what she's going to do in this picture. Now lookit. The Duchess of Richmond—"

"Excuse me," said Monica, worming past them.

Controlling herself, she followed the boy along the aisle. But the sight of those two brought back the certainty that she *had* seen the page-boy somewhere before, and somewhere in connection with them.

The boy, making a motorist's turn signal with his hand, abruptly pivoted to the left and led the way into a kind of long cavern. Far away, near the entrance of the sound stage, Monica could see a small crowd of workmen going out, and hear the ring of a time-clock being punched. She hoped uneasily that everybody was not going away and leaving her.

She overtook the boy.

"Listen to me, please," she said sharply. "Where is Mr. Hackett?"

"Dunno, miss," said the boy, flinging his head round in true parade-ground style, and flinging it back again.

"But didn't you say he gave you a message for me?"

"Bulletin board, miss."

"What?"

"Bulletin board, miss."

"And *where* did you say we were going? Practical house on Eighteen-eight-something?"

"They calls it Eighteen-eighty-two," said the boy, wearily imparting information, " 'Cos that's the date the pitcher was supposed to be in. It was a costume

65

pitcher. It was about a doctor that was a murderer. Here yar, miss. Albion Films Service. Good day."

Then Monica recognized the long, dim set on which they were standing.

It was the replica of a suburban street, which had been constructed indoors for the filming of a story by William Cartwright. Cartwright had pointed it out to her half an hour ago. Seen close at hand, it became a lifelike and rather creepy-looking place. The street, with houses on both sides, was built of cobblestones in some grayish plaster composition. Though most of the houses were dummy fronts, one of them—the doctor's—had been built and furnished throughout.

Distant lights cast a dim reflection along the tops of them, making the upstairs windows wink and turning the gray fronts bluish. Below, it was so dark that Monica had to grope her way. Not a soul stirred in it. The "practical" house, presumably, was the doctor's. This was a little low doll's house of a place, a gray stone front, with bow-windows above and below. Frilled lace curtains were chastely drawn at the windows. Beside the door, which had an antique bell-pull and two steps leading up to it, was a brass plate inscribed *Dr. Rodman Teriss, M.D.*

Of all the queer places for Mr. Hackett to choose, this was the queerest. Monica turned to the boy.

"But why—"

The page-boy was gone.

She walked up the two steps to the doctor's door. On an experimental impulse she pulled at the brass knob of the bell, and was instantly answered by a long cowbell jangle which made her nerves jump.

Realistic, too, was the blistered paint of the door. She touched the door, and it swung open.

Inside was a little hall, so thickly stuffy that it was difficult to breathe. In the dimness she could just make out a staircase rising along the wall to the right, and on the left the doors to the two downstairs rooms.

"Hello!" she called.

There was no reply. Monica, hesitating on the step, felt a faint twinge of alarm, an irrational stir at the nerves. But she knew this to be nonsense. She was not entering a lonely house in a suburban street at midnight. She was entering a painted film set, constructed in the middle of a big barn where people were moving and talking and laughing all around her.

She walked into the little hall, and two steps took her through an open door into the front room. Here she barked her ankle against a chair. She was not frightened, but she suddenly felt furiously angry with Thomas Hackett for all this foolishness. Why couldn't they say what they wanted? Why did they have to do things like this?

There was a box of matches in her handbag. She got it out and struck a match. The brief flame showed her a room so completely furnished, so realistically arranged, that she was almost shocked: as though she had blundered into a real house.

There were just such rooms round about East Roystead. It breathed the atmosphere of the nineteenth century. Mr. Lensworth, the dentist at Ridley, had a waiting-room very much like it. There was a heavy reddish cloth, with tassels, on the center table; and antimacassars over the chairs. That picture over the mantelpiece — "The Banjo Player" — she had seen many times at her Grandmother Styles's.

The match went out. Then she saw that there was a door at the back of the room, and that under this door wavered a thin, yellow line of light.

In the back room, Mr. Hackett had said. She stumbled across to this door, and opened it.

A real gas-jet was burning, bluish yellow, inside a flattish shade like a glass dish. It was set on a bracket over a roll-top desk, and the dim flame wavered with the opening of the door. The room was small and dingy, with cracked linoleum on the floor. A stethoscope and a dresser's case lay on the center table. The shelf of the portentous black mantelpiece was strewn with cotton wadding and bandages, glass measures, thermometers, and syringes. From one wall projected the metal mouth of a speaking-tube — by which, presumably, the doctor's wife could communicate with him from the room above. Below this were shelves lined with bottles and books. There were a couple of plush chairs, and a rather gruesome anatomical chart.

But there was nobody here.

The dim light glistened on the bottles, on the maplewood desk, and on the metal mouth of the speaking-tube.

Reassuringly, she could look out of a broad rear window, dusty but uncurtained, into the gloom of the sound-stage. This was only make-believe. Half of her mind admired the unpleasantly realistic detail. But the other half began to be infected with a tinge of pure superstitious terror. She had been through a number of emotional crises that day, and she had eaten nothing since breakfast. Imagination, always vivid, joined with memories of childhood: it fastened on this room and peopled the sweating walls. She wondered what 'Dr. Rodman Teriss, M.D.' had done. She wondered what she would do if that cupboard opened, and somebody walked out.

Over her head, a board in the ceiling creaked slightly, and creaked again.

There was somebody walking about in the room above.

If this were a practical joke of some kind, Monica swore she would make someone pay for it. Had Thomas Hackett sent that message after all? Was the detestable Cartwright up to something, which he might think was funny?

Between anger and nervousness and the stifling heat of the room, she felt the perspiration start out on her body. Her heart was thudding, and (most annoying of all) as a climax to the day she found tears of pure nerves stinging into her eyes.

"Hel-lo!" she cried, forcing speech at the top of her lungs. *"Who is it? Where are you?*

Across the room the speaking-tube whistled.

So it was a joke. A damnable and detestable piece of clowning on somebody's part.

"I can hear you up there!" she shouted. "Come down! I know you're there."

The speaking-tube whistled again.

It could no more be ignored than a ringing telephone. It stung her and drew her from mingled curiosity and rage. She flew at it.

"If you think this is funny," she said into the mouth of the tube, "just come down here and I'll tell you different. Who are you? What do you want?"

She bent her cheek to the mouth of the tube to listen for an answer. And in the same moment she became aware of two things.

Standing sideways to the mouth of the tube, she was looking obliquely out of the large rear window. Even in the dim, flickering pin-point of the gas-jet, she could see William Cartwright outside. He was standing motionless, looking straight into her eyes from a distance of fifteen feet away, and on his face there was a look of horror. In the same instant, coming to life, Cartwright flung back his arm and threw something straight at her face.

Monica's movement was instinctive. She leaped back, dodging and crying out. A lump of putty, weighing perhaps a quarter of a pound, smashed the windowpane with a bursting crash, thudded against the side wall, and ricocheted among bottles. As Monica jumped back, something happened to the speaking-tube.

Something which looked like water, but was not water, spurted in a jet from the mouth of the tube. It passed exactly across the place where Monica's cheek and eyes had been pressed half a second before. The first jet splashed across the linoleum; the speaking-tube gurgled like a pipe, sputtering, and gushed again.

A pungent odor scraped the nostrils in that hot room. Smoke, light and acrid, blossomed in little white dots on the linoleum; and there was a hissing, sizzling noise as half a pint of vitriol, poured down a speaking-tube as though down a large pipe, began to eat into the surface of the floor.

The footsteps in the room above began to run.

Monica was not sick.

She thought she was going to be, but she was not. It was perhaps twenty seconds before she realized what had happened, and by that time Cartwright was with her.

Cartwright, his face as white as paper, reached through the broken window, caught hold of the sash, and pushed it up. His hand was shaking so much that he cut it on ragged glass, but he did not notice this. Hauling himself up with easy agility, he swung himself into the room; slipped, and almost fell forward into the smoking pool.

"Did it touch you?" she heard his voice saying. It sounded very far away. "Any of it? A drop, even?"

Monica shook her head.

"Are you sure? Not a drop? Look out! — don't step in it! Sure?"

Monica nodded violently.

"Move over here. God, I'll kill somebody for this! Easy, now. What happened?"

"U-upstairs," said Monica. "He p-poured it—"

"I know."

"You know? No, don't go up there!" She was clinging to his sleeve. She felt her fingernails scrape on the rough cloth. Though she had said no acid had touched her, she was terrified for fear it had after all; momentarily she expected to feel the bite and burn of it on her body. "Don't, please don't!"

He shook off her hand and ran for the door opening from the office into the hall. Footsteps, at a running tiptoe, went stealthily down the staircase out in the hall. Outside, only a few yards away, ran the person who had poured the acid. And the office door was locked on the outside.

Cartwright turned and plunged into the dark front room. As he did so the outer door of the doctor's house closed softly. With Monica following him in a state close to hysteria, he reached the front door and stared up and down the mimic street.

It was empty.

V

William Cartwright walked slowly back to the doctor's consulting-room. He looked round him. The acid had almost ceased to sizzle, though the reek of it was still hot. He looked at the lump of putty, lying on the floor amid fragments of bottles it had knocked off the shelf. He passed his hand across his forehead. But all he said was:

"It's a good thing I had that putty."

"If it hadn't been for you, I should have been—"

"Steady! And, anyway, I didn't mean that!"

"S-sorry. I can't help it."

"A jolt of brandy would do you good, young lady. Come on: let's go and see if we can find one."

Monica would not be diverted. "But how did you know?" she insisted. "I mean, how did you think to throw the putty at me? How did you know what was happening?"

"Because I am responsible for this?"

"Responsible?"

Cartwright's manner was full of a sardonic bitterness which at any other time she would have thought ridiculous. He would not meet her eye.

"I invented the device," he answered, nodding toward the speaking-tube. "That neat little device, which almost caught you, was my idea. We used it in the film about the doctor." He paused, moving his neck. "In the depths of my prophetic soul, I can swear I was afraid something like this might happen. Do you remember—ten or fifteen minutes ago—when Tom Hackett shouted to Howard Fisk and me, and asked us to come over and join him? We left you with Frances?"

"Yes."

Cartwright looked at the speaking-tube.

"It was to report," he said, "that nearly a quart of sulphuric acid had been stolen from the head electrician's stock."

"Yes?"

"Well, only a pint of it had been used to put in that water-bottle on the other set. We naturally wanted to know what had happened to the rest of it. Since somebody seemed to have a fondness for sulphuric acid, it was worth looking into. Even the Jovian-browed Howard was a little disturbed. They decided they wouldn't do any more shooting that day, and dismissed the technical staff for the afternoon."

"I remember. I saw them go."

"Then the rest of us separated, and started out on a hunt to find out what had happened to the rest of the acid. I know what *I* did: I came over here. When I saw a light in that window, I was afflicted with a sudden feeling of the heebie-jeebies. When I saw you standing by that tube, with the side of your face against it—"

Again Cartwright paused. Monica regarded him with real horror.

"You say you invented the t-trick of pouring acid down a speaking-tube."

"I did."

"You know," Monica breathed, "you're not safe to have about. You ought to be locked up. You're dangerous."

"All right, all right! *Peccavi* and *mea* ruddy *culpa*," said Cartwright. He lifted his hands, crooked the forefingers at the temples, and moved them in the air. "Behold the lineaments of Satan. Dirty tricks to order; murderous devices designed, delivered, and guaranteed by William Cartwright, Esq. I own the error and will endeavor to starve in the future. Does that satisfy you?"

"And you've cut your hand!"

"Be good enough, madam, to let my hand alone."

"Oh, don't be so absurd!"

Drawing a deep breath, Cartwright took up a careful stance like a man about to play a golf-stroke, and folded his hands carefully behind his back.

"And now," he said, "will you kindly tell me what you are doing here?"

Monica told him. She was at that state of affairs where she had to burst out with it or die. Cartwright regarded her incredulously.

"Tom Hackett sent you that message?"

"That's what the page-boy said. I don't believe it either, but — "

"Did he *see* Tom?"

"I don't know. I asked him where Mr. Hackett was, and he said he didn't know. He also said something about a bulletin board."

"So that's it!"

"What is it? What are you talking about?"

Cartwright stared at vacancy. "It's the black-board," he answered, coming out of his trance, "just inside the entrance to the sound-stage. Did you notice it?"

"No."

"A page-boy sits by the door and keeps guard. He's theoretically supposed to let people in and out. But he also runs errands and takes messages, though he isn't allowed out of the stage. When he happens to be gone for a minute or two, and you want something done, you just take a piece of chalk and write your instructions on the blackboard.

"Don't you see it? When the page wasn't there, somebody walked calmly up and wrote, *'Please tell Miss Stanton to—'* and the rest of it; signed, *T. Hackett*. He could have turned out the little lamp over the blackboard, and not a soul would have seen him. I'll bet you a fiver that's what happened.

"Then the person was all prepared. He came here and lit the gas snugly and cozily. He went upstairs with his bottle of vitriol. He knew you would come to this room. He knew you would answer the speaking-tube. And the worst of it is that the swine got the whole idea from me."

Monica moved back until she was touching the wall.

This wasn't happening. It couldn't be.

Her mind held a vivid picture of what would have happened if Cartwright had not flung that lump of putty and made her jump back. But revulsion was kept back by bewilderment. She felt as though the room were beginning to stifle her; as, in a literal sense, it was.

"But who—"

"I don't know," said Cartwright, rubbing the side of his beard. "I don't know."

"And why? I mean, why *me?*" (This was the staggering injustice.) "Why should anybody do that to me? I h-haven't done anything to anybody. I don't even know anybody here!"

"Steady, now."

"It was a mistake, don't you see? It must have been. That message must have been meant for somebody else. And yet I don't see how it could have been. The boy said 'Miss Stanton.' He said it distinctly."

"Careful," Cartwright said sharply. "There's somebody coming."

He made a quick gesture. A noise of quick, firm footsteps approached outside the shattered window. In the dim gas-light, wavering with any movement, a part of a head appeared above the windowsill. It consisted of hair, forehead, eyes, and the upper part of a nose. The eyes, light blue and glistening where the dim light caught their whites, looked steadily at them.

"I thought I heard a loud noise," the newcomer observed. "Is anything wrong?"

Cartwright grunted.

"You did hear a loud noise," he said. "You heard it like blazes. Excuse me. This is . . . by the way, what do I call you? Mr. Gagern? Herr Gagern? Or Baron von Gagern?

2

The appearance of that half-face, cut off by the window ledge just below the eyes, had made Monica press back: not because the newcomer was alarming, but because he was unfamiliar. The newcomer's fresh complexion gave him a look of youthfulness. But the straw-colored hair, parted at one side and brushed flat round his head, had begun to turn dry and gray at the temples. There were long, fine, horizontal wrinkles in his forehead. His English was not only good; it was flawless, though slow-spoken.

"Please call me what you like," he replied seriously. "I should prefer Mr. Gagern, I think."

"Mr. Gagern, this is Miss Stanton."

The eyes at the window shifted sideways. There was a noise of invisible heels being clicked together.

"Miss Stanton has just found the acid," added Cartwright.

"I do not understand what you mean."

"Come in here and you will. Somebody worked the same dodge that was used in *The Doctor's Pleasure*. Somebody brought Miss Stanton here with a fake message, poured acid down that speaking-tube, and got away. Except for a lucky accident, she wouldn't be talking to us now."

Gagern changed color like a schoolboy. Then he turned his back to the window and shouted, "Here! This way!"

It was surprising how quiet, in the past minutes,

the whole sound-stage had become. You missed the eternal tinkling background, the ghost of noises. Though not loud, Gagern's voice rang out and reverberated, the echoes falling down from the roof like wooden blocks dislodged. There was a stir of footsteps hurrying from some distance away.

But Gagern was not so undignified as to climb through the window. He walked clear around the set and came in at the front door.

Cartwright told him what had happened.

"I don't like this," said Gagern, shaking his head.

"I, on the other hand," Cartwright said through his teeth, "do like it. I like it fine. It's my idea of a perfect day."

"No, I mean that it is not good sense. That is what troubles me."

"Miss Stanton was also a little troubled."

"Yes. Forgive me," said Gagern seriously.

He turned to Monica, clicked his heels again, and smiled. He had an unexpected and wholly attractive smile. It suddenly lighted and lightened his face, making him seem a dozen years younger and obscuring the traces of gray in his smooth yellow hair. Kurt von Gagern was a wiry, middle-sized man with a blue sweater and a cricket shirt open at the neck. His manner was punctilious. Yet Monica, super-sensitive to atmospheres, felt either that he was not sure of something in his own mind or that there was something not quite right about him. His hands were encased in dark kid gloves; and with these he made a gesture, palms upward.

"It is not that I am unsympathetic," he explained, "but that I am disturbed."

"Please don't mention it."

"Your experience was not a happy one. At the same time"—the blue eyes shifted toward Cartwright—"you say, sir, that you saw it happen?"

"I did."

"You perhaps saw the person who poured the acid? Through the upstairs window?"

"No. The room upstairs was dark."

"That is unfortunate." Gagern shook his head. "Very unfortunate." He shook his head again. "Did you see anyone hanging about the place? Or get a glimpse of any person running away?"

"No, I didn't. Did you?"

"I beg your pardon?"

"I said, did you? You were here very promptly after it. So I just wondered whether you did."

Though Cartwright's tone was casual, he had perhaps not such a good poker-face as he would have liked everybody to believe. Since Gagern's entrance, Cartwright had been eyeing him with such a fixed and unwavering stare that the earnest Teuton was beginning to fidget under it. Gagern's color came and went again. He did not seem to know what to do with his gloved hands.

Gagern evidently decided that this was a joke.

"I saw nobody," he smiled, "except my wife. She had taken a short-cut through the street of Eighteen-eighty-two, and had broken off the heel of her slipper in a cobblestone.

"I didn't mean Frances."

"Then be pleased to tell me what you did mean."

"Nothing, nothing!"

A new sensation, as unpleasant in suggestion as

the instruments in the mimic doctor's office, had begun to creep into this room. Cartwright was saved the necessity of replying by Mr. Thomas Hackett, who entered with a masterful but distressed air through the front door and the waiting-room.

Mr. Hackett took one look at the acid stains on the floor, and sniffed the odor of burnt metal from the speaking-tube. His swarthy face looked slightly ill; it became very ill before Cartwright had finished telling him the story.

"Stop a bit, stop a bit!" he urged, making a mesmeric pass under his informant's nose. "When did this happen?"

Cartwright consulted a wrist-watch. "It happened at just ten minutes past five. True to my professional training, I can tell you to a minute. Why?"

"But that's impossible. Now, Bill—!"

"I tell you it was ten minutes past five. Can't you fix the time for yourself? Didn't you hear that window smash with a noise to wake the dead? That was when it happened."

Mr. Hackett reflected. "Yes, that's true. But it's still impossible."

"Why?"

"Because," replied the producer, "there's nobody here except you and Miss Stanton and Frances and Kurt and Howard and myself. Everybody else has left for the day."

Cartwright shut his eyes, and opened them again. "Are you sure of that? Positive?"

"Oh, Lord, am I sure? I watched 'em go out. I stood by the sound-stage door and counted 'em when they went. Don't you see, I had to make sure nobody

81

sneaked a bottle of acid out of the place? Howard dismissed the technical unit at just on five o'clock. The make-up man, and Jay Harned—he's acting for the continuity girl, who's away today—and Dick Conyers, and Annie MacPherson, and Frances's maid went with 'em. Everybody else employed here, the workmen are all trade-union men and had to clock out at five anyway. I'd already chased out visitors (did you notice?) and had the place searched to make sure there was nobody here. The sliding doors were already locked—"

"But why the elaborate precautions?"

"Sabotage, my lad. Sabotage, or I'll eat my hat. The last people to go were old Aaronson and Van Ghent of Radiant Pictures, who wandered in here. I couldn't very well throw *them* out, but they left by five minutes past five. Then I set the sound-recording lock on the door. There's not as much as a ghost in this place except the six of us. Bill, you must be mistaken about the time!"

"The time," returned Cartwright stolidly, "was ten minutes past five." He turned to Gagern. "Don't you agree?"

Gagern shook his head.

"I regret to say that I did not consult my watch. But I agree that I think it must have been approximately ten minutes past five."

"Wait a minute," said Cartwright. "there's another thing, Tom. What about the page-boy?"

"Eh?"

"Jimmy Whatshisname. The page-boy at the entrance. Did he go with the rest of them?"

"Yes. He—"

Mr. Hackett paused. He had lifted a broad, stubby-fingered hand, and was nervously rubbing his blue chin and smoothing down his toothbrush mustache. Recollection came into his eyes. He snapped his fingers.

"Got it!" he said. "I knew there was something else. If you want to see the top peak and crown of this whole business, come along. Come with me."

Monica was glad enough to get out of that toy house. She had an impluse to take hold of Cartwright's arm; and, firmly conquering this, she put herself on the other side of Mr. Hackett. The producer led the way at a rapid, knees-out stride like a long-distance walker. The immensity of the silence was emphasized by the rattling of their footfalls on imitation cobblestones; it was weirdly like the noise of horses' hoofs. Monica wished Mr. Hackett would not talk so much.

"Kurt. Look. Will you go and find Frances? And Howard? I don't know where they are. There's probably somebody hidden somewhere. Must be. Will you? There's a good fellow. You others—here."

He swung round when they reached the entrance-door. It was built in the form of a box or compartment, with two doors to exclude sound. Round one corner was a workmen's time-clock, with the hands at twenty minutes past five. At the other corner was a row of pigeon-holes full of papers below a small blackboard. In the gloom Monica could make out no more than outlines, until Mr. Hackett switched on a small lamp above the blackboard.

Written across it in chalk were the straggling words, "Tell the lady with Mr. Cartwright to meet me in the back room of the practical house, 1882, at once. Thos. Hackett."

And Thos. Hackett cleared his throat.

"You see it?" he demanded.

"I see it," Cartwright said grimly. "You didn't write it?"

"No, no, certainly not!"

"But, if you were standing by the door more or less from five o'clock on, you must have seen who did write it?"

Mr. Hackett considered this. He kept his finger on the blackboard under the words, and craned his neck round. His hair, black and ridged, shone under the light as though there were vaseline on it.

"Well, I didn't see who did it. Come to think of it, why should I have? I was standing over at the other side, by the time-clock. I don't even remember noticing the board, or whether the light was on over it. Besides, how do we know when it was written?"

"Yes; but when did you first see the message?"

"Only a few minutes ago, just before I heard somebody yell from the direction of Eighteen-eighty-two, — Who yelled, by the way?"

"Gagern."

"I thought so." The other nodded. "I heard the window smash, right enough. But at that time I was clear over at the far end of the floor, looking for the rest of you; and I couldn't tell where the noise came from. I walked back here, to see if any of you were at the door. I put the light on, and there the message was. Directly afterwards, Gagern gave a shout. it was easy to trace that. Not that I thought there was anything wrong, mind! After all, there are only—"

He stopped.

"Yes," agreed Cartwright. "There are only the six of us here."

Hollow, very distant, tinny-sounding as though through a far-off amplifier, Gagern's voice rose for the second time through the sound-stage. It made them all jump. What it cried was:

"Mr. Hackett! If you please! Come here! My wife has been hurt."

The producer moistened his lips. "That's done it," he said, after a pause while the echoes thundered. He passed the back of his hand across his forehead. "It only wanted that, didn't it? It's sabotage, and you know it as well as I do."

"Don't rub out that writing," snarled Cartwright, as his companion made an instinctive gesture. "That's a real clue. That's handwriting. It can be identified."

"Damn the handwriting," said Mr. Hackett. "Come on."

But, when they arrived breathless at the cabin of the ocean liner, where welcome lights glowed, they found nothing very alarming. Howard Fisk, tall and mild and paternal (not to say motherly), tried to clear his throat for audible speech. Frances Fleur, an expression of annoyance marring her placid face, was sitting on a camp-stool and vigorously rubbing her knee.

"Kurt, I wish you wouldn't make all this fuss," she protested. "It's nothing at all. Only a bruise." She appealed to the others. "I broke the heel off one of my shoes, and I was foolish enough to try to walk on it afterwards. I fell, Honestly, Kurt —"

"My dear, you may say so. But I have known such bruises to have very serious consequences. I have known them to end in cancer, even. I think we should send for the doctor."

"Kurt, darling, it's nothing! Look."

"My dear, I beg of you not to do that, before all these people. It is immodest."

"Very well, darling."

Howard Fisk, who did not seem impressed by this, nevertheless showed a state of uneasiness which made him audible at ten feet.

"Yes, yes," he said. "Too bad, no doubt. But we seem to have run into something that's a good deal worse than a bruise. Look here. Hackett. Miss Stanton. Is it true, what Gagern has been telling us? About that confounded acid?"

"I'm afraid it is," said Monica.

"But who in the name of sense would want to make an attack on *your* life?"

There was a silence, during which they all looked at Monica. Kurt Gagern was standing behind Frances Fleur's chair. Monica was astounded to see him bend over and press his lips to his wife's shoulder.

"It's sabotage, I tell you," said Mr. Hackett. He seemed flattered and, in a dim sort of way, almost pleased. "I've been half expecting something like this ever since we started making *Spies at Sea*. Remember what happened in Hollywood when they made that first anti-Nazi picture? This film is just a little too strong for 'em, that's what it is. Look at all the aliens in this country! Swarms of 'em! There must be hundreds of secret spies planted in the middle of us. (No reference to you, of course, Kurt.) They didn't like it.

86

So—"

"So," interrupted Howard Fisk, "they tried to blind and maim a complete stranger, a girl who had nothing whatever to do with the film?"

"Certainly."

"But why?"

"So that we'd get the police in here, and work would have to stop on *Spies at Sea*. And, by jingo, I'm going to see that we don't get the police in here."

"But, my dear Hackett," expostulated the director, "that isn't reasonable. Even if you did call the police, that would not stop work on *Spies at Sea*."

"It wouldn't?

"No; why should it? Miss Stanton has no connection with the film. There mere presence of police here on the floor wouldn't hold up the making of a film which was no concern of theirs. And if your theoretical saboteur wanted to ditch *Spies at Sea* by throwing acid at somebody, why not make a real job of it by throwing acid at a leading member of the cast?"

Again there was a silence.

During this exchange, William Cartwright had not spoken. In defiance of the regulation against smoking, he had filled and lighted his Sherlock Holmes pipe. But he went unnoticed.

"It comes down to this," declared Fisk, after some slow-motion thought. "Whatever happened, the question is: why should anybody want to attack Miss Stanton?" He looked round. "You don't know of anybody who would . . . er . . . want to hurt you, do you?"

"No, I swear I don't!"

"You never saw anybody here before today?"

"Never."

The director smiled. "And you don't know any Official Secrets, or dangerous information about anybody?"

"Not a one."

The director strolled over towards her. Monica felt that if he put his arm round her and bent over confidentially, as he seemed about to do, she would give a yell. Kurt Gagern's pale blue eyes were also fixed on her, the whites glistening where the light caught them. Monica felt that her nerves were being sawed in two—with long, slow rasps of the saw.

"Then there's nothing else for it," said Fisk, lifting his large shoulders. "This thing's too ugly to be a practical joke." Disturbed, he touched his pince-nez. "Either this was the work of a criminal lunatic; or else, as seems most likely, Miss Stanton was summoned there in mistake for somebody else."

"No," said William Cartwright.

They all shouted at him, but he held up his hand.

"There was no mistake," he went on. "And, disregarding the fact that the page-boy obviously got the right person, I will tell you why there wasn't." He took the pipe out of his mouth, and looked at Monica. "That street outside the doctor's house—it was darkish, wasn't it?"

"Yes, of course."

"But not too dark? For instance, you could easily read the name on the doctor's brass plate?"

"Yes; I remember doing that."

"And you'd have recognized anybody you met at, say, ten or twelve feet?"

"Yes, I think I should have."

Again Cartwright shouted down protests. "The swine who did this," he went on, "we'll call, for the sake of convenience, the murderer. Now, this was no accident. The murderer deliberately arranged everything. He was waiting for her. He saw her approach, by the simple process of looking out of the upstairs window in a little low doll's house not nine feet over her head. He had to know who was there before he could act. Right?"

Mr. Hackett boiled. "Oh, for the love of Mike cut out the detective-story methods! What do you mean?"

"*I'm* not using detective-story methods," said Cartwright. "The murderer did that. All right. How many women were there on the set this afternoon?"

"There were four," Howard Fisk answered thoughtfully. "Apart from Miss Stanton, three. Frances, Frances's maid, and Annie MacPherson."

"Only those?"

"Only those."

"Yes. And each of those three, if you remember, had a distinctive costume which couldn't be mistaken. Frances wore that noble gold evening dress you see there. MacPherson wore the stewardess's white uniform and white cap. Frances's maid wore the conventional cap and apron. Apart from the fact that none of them looks like Monica Stanton, or is built like her, it is absolutely impossible for any of them to have been mistaken for that girl there. For some reason I don't understand, the murderer hates her beyond reason; and that acid-pouring business was the result."

Howard Fisk scratched the back of his neck.

"H'm," he said.

"Thank God it wasn't me," Frances Fleur said suddenly. She corrected herself and smiled at Monica. "I mean—not that I *wanted* it to be you, my dear. But vitriol! Ugh!"

"That is understandable," agreed Gagern, shifting uneasily from one foot to the other. "I do not often agree with you, Mr. Cartwright. At times I find your notions wild and foolish and not good screen material either. But I confess you seem to have the right on your side in this instance."

"Thanks."

"I spoke in good faith, Mr. Cartwright," rapped Gagern, drawing his heels together. "At the same time, is it necessary to frighten Miss Stanton more than she has been frightened?"

The intolerable Cartwright then reached his lowest level.

"Frighten her?" he said. "If that will do any good, yes. I'm so jittery over this thing myself that I can't hold a pipe straight. Aren't any of the rest of you? Frighten her? What I want to do is persuade her to get away from Pineham and stay away, in case the same merry joker tries it again"

"I'll do no such thing!" cried Monica. Yet she felt fear take hold of her heart, and squeeze hard.

"Just as you like, then."

"If," said Monica, "you want to drive me away so that you can write your ridiculous, silly, detective story yourself—"

An hour ago, she would not have regretted saying a thing like that. Now, the moment the words were out of her mouth, she wished she could have recalled

90

them. Damn! Double damn!

Cartwright did not say anything. He looked at her steadily, and then sat down in a camp-chair and puffed furiously at the curved pipe.

"Yes, that's all very well," grumbled Mr. Hackett. "This is all wrong. I thought there might be a fine newspaper story in this. But it's nothing; it's just bad publicity. The point is, what are we going to do?"

"Don't ask me," said Cartwright. "You are the Lords of the Thousand Lamps. I am only one of the writers, the lowest of crawling creatures about a film-studio."

(Now he's sulking, drat him!)

"Yes, I know that," agreed Mr. Hackett seriously: "but you claim to know something about it. What in blazes are we going to do?"

"You might begin," said Cartwright, "by finding out which one of us was the joker who poured the acid."

"Of us?"

"Naturally."

Four voices rose and rang out and reverberated under the barn in protest. To speak more correctly, three voices did: for nobody could hear what Howard Fisk said. But it was the director who took command of the situation.

"There's reason in what Cartwright says," he smiled. "Oh, yes, there is! We know it's all nonsense, of course, but let's give it fair consideration."

"Let's search the place. That's more likely," snapped Mr. Hackett, rolling his eyes. "There's somebody hidden here. You know it. I know it. Any other idea—"

"And I suppose we ought to begin," said the director, "by accounting to each other for our movements at the time this thing happened. The alibi. That's the proper formula, isn't it? Come on, my young Thorndyke: isn't that the first question a real detective would ask?"

"I do not suppose," observed Gagern smilingly, "that Mr. Cartwright by any chance knows any real detectives?"

Cartwright looked up.

"I have the honor," he replied, imitating Gagern's style, "to know only one. His name is Masters, and he's a chief inspector of the C.I.D. Heaven willing, I mean to talk this over with him in private. It would also be interesting to hear the opinion of a great friend of his in Whitehall, whom I don't know."

"No sidetracking!" said Mr. Fisk. "The alibi. Isn't that the first question a real detective would ask?"

"No," said Cartwright.

"It isn't?"

"I doubt it." Cartwright shifted round. He contemplated the bedroom of the luxury liner, more subdued now under fewer lights, but still polished with its colors of white and pink and gold. A whiff of smoke from his pipe floated out across it.

"A real detective," he added, "would probably ask who designed that set."

"What?"

Gagern spoke in a puzzled voice. "The set was reconstructed from photographs, as the custom is. Since it was to be a German liner, we used photographs of the *Brünhilde*. I supervised the arrangement."

"As the custom is," said Cartwright.

Gagern stepped round from behind his wife's chair. She pressed his hand and gave him a glance as he moved, and he smiled in reply. His expression was less of guilt than of acute embarrassment, not unmixed with exasperation.

"Mr. Cartwright," he said, "I have attempted to be patient with you. Have you any complaint to make of me?"

"Of you? No."

Gagern blinked. "Then — ?"

"I only say," declared Cartwright, "that I smell blood on that set and that the joker who stole the vitriol won't stop at one go."

"It pleases you to be fanciful."

"It pleases me to ruddy well tell the truth."

"Kurt," said Frances Fleur, "he means it. I know him. There's something he knows and won't tell us."

She had a fine contralto voice, which she rarely raised. It was the voice that strikes notes off glass; it was badly trained, but expressive beyond the range of her acting powers. It rose clearly in the hot, dim shed: amused, cheerful, but faintly apprehensive. She said, taking her husband's hand:

"Nothing's going to happen; is it, Kurt?"

3

This was on Wednesday, the twenty-third of August. Before a fortnight had elapsed, there was a new noise in the earth. The dozenth pledge was broken, the gray mass burst loose; over London the sirens roared as the Prime Minister finished speaking; the great concrete hats of the Maginot Line revolved, and looked toward the West; Poland died, with all her guns still ablaze; the nights of the blackouts came; and at Pineham, a small spot in England, a patient murderer struck again at Monica Stanton.

VI

It was past seven o'clock — blacking-out time.

Since nobody could take a holiday, the September weather was fine and mellow. Pineham drowsed toward dusk, its buildings full of a silence which indicated that the film business had come almost to a standstill.

The President of the Board of Trade had announced that he meant to repeal the Film Quota Act, which meant that the American companies could no longer profitably make pictures in England. Twenty out of twenty-six film studios had been commandeered for "storage" and other purposes. Petrol was going to be difficult to get, and so was timber: the most important necessity in film-making.

But there were a few (gradually becoming the many) who were not affrighted. Independent units were picking up. Radiant Pictures went ahead to finish *Iron Duke*. And Mr. Thomas Hackett, backed by the mysterious Mr. Marshlake, announced that he would do more than finish his film *Spies at Sea,* which had now become red-hot propaganda. Since several of the sound stages were rescued, he would go straight ahead with his production schedule until somebody strangled him.

At the Old Building, idyllic calm reigned. On the ground floor, overlooking the lake, literary inspiration was at work. Here were three little white-painted offices, all in a line. Each office had a tiny cloakroom, with wash-basin and gas-ring. Each office had a door communicating with the next one, and another door giving on the central corridor. Each office had a chair, a desk, a typewriter, a sofa, and an occupant.

In the first office sat the scenario expert from Hollywood, busily engaged in knocking the stuffing out of the original script of *Spies at Sea,* and rewriting about half of it. In the second office sat Monica Stanton, engaged in learning how to manipulate a typewriter while she plodded away at a detective story. And in the third office sat William Cartwright, not at the moment engaged in anything.

Mr. Cartwright brooded.

He sat back and stared at the keys of the typewriter. He stared at the long row of pipes — every variety of pipe, from a light little brier to a noble meerschaum shaped like a skull — which lay along his desk. But they brought him no consolation. He thrust his hands into the pockets of his coat, and stared distastefully at the ceiling. Finally, unable to bear it, he smote the desk a whack with his fist and got up.

It was intolerable.

Why, in the midst of all these other perplexities, had he got to go and fall in love with the damned girl?

The Old Building was very quiet. From the other two communicating offices he could hear a noise of typewriters which was characteristic. First there would be Tilly Parson's typewriter: rattling away in sudden rapid bursts like a machine-gun, with long pauses between. Then there would be Monica Stanton's: mostly pauses in hard hits, but with an abrupt pick-up towards the end of the line, a pause, and then a decisive *plop* to mark the full-stop. That plop had a triumphant air, as of something achieved.

He looked at the white door—closed—which separated them. At least she had left no doubt in anybody's mind as to how she felt toward him.

"She loathes you, Bill," Frances had assured him, laughing. "She told me so herself. What on earth did you do to her, the first time you two met? It must have been something rather awful, if you know what I mean."

"I didn't do anything."

"Come on, now, Bill! Tell Frances. What was it?"

And Howard Fisk had been almost as definite.

"To tell you the truth, my lad," the director had confided, "I think it's your beard. I asked her the other day how she would like to be kissed by a man with a beard—"

"What in hell did you do that for?"

"Oh, tut, tut! Why are you writer blokes so touchy? I didn't mean anything. I was wondering whether we'd better have Dick Conyers wear a naval beard in the fight sequences, and how the women would react to it. Still, if you don't want to hear—"

"Sorry. What did she say?"

"She didn't say anything. She just shuddered. It started inside her and went all over her, as though she'd picked up a spider."

As though she had picked up a spider, eh?

William Cartwright, at this time, was not feeling any more popular with himself than he appeared to be with Monica Stanton. Like most of us in those early days, he was feeling restless. His persistent attempts to get into the Army had met with no success whatever. In his heart he admired the calm, deadly efficiency with which the Government were forcing the war, like a game of chess, to an inevitable end; without flags, without flurry, taking not one more untrained man than they needed. He knew that his best policy was to stop fidgeting and wait to be called up.

But there it was.

In the second place, he figured at Pineham as a cashiered prophet. Nothing of a murderous nature had happened. Life went on as cheerfully as anywhere else in England, though lashed to high pressure by Mr. Hackett. For the blacked-out nights, when people groped and stumbled and swore and made jokes in every street of the land, Tom Hackett had devised for himself a costume consisting of a coat with luminous buttons, and a luminous hat. It made him resemble something imagined by Mr. H. G. Wells, and was not a sight for weak nerves.

Since petrol rationing would shortly come in, most

of the crowd were living either at the Merefield Country Club, or in cottages and lodgings near the studios. Kurt Gagern, in the course of directing a submarine scene in the lake, fell overboard and was confined to bed with 'flu. Many of the younger men had been called up; one quiet electrician sported, surprisingly, the three stars of a captain.

And into the middle of it, chuckling, talking endlessly, laying down the law, plunged Tilly Parsons.

"The highest-paid scenario-writer in the world" was a little, dumpy, bustling woman in her early fifties. She had a flat positiveness of manner which carried everybody along with her. Though her lipstick always looked as though it had been put on in the dark, so that it was just a fraction of an inch sideways across her mouth, she had a good deal of charm. She was always talking of slimming, and ordered horrible concoctions in the Pineham restaurant.

"Lamb chops and pineapple," she declared, in a hoarse cigarette voice which swept the tables like the blare of a corn-crake. "That's the stuff, honey. Dalmatia Divine used it in the old silent days, and it's never been beat yet. She came down from a hundred and forty-six to a hundred and eighteen, whango! — in two weeks. I'll do it too. You see. I always do it when I work."

And she was working.

She first took the script of *Spies at Sea,* and went into a trance with it. She then informed Mr. Hackett — to his gratification — that it was terrible but that she thought she could fix it. Despite the prayers and curses of both Howard Fisk and William Cartwright, she was encouraged to do this.

Then she got down to business. Brewing endless pots of coffee on the gas-ring in the cloak-room, and smoking Chesterfields until the office was blue, she began the revisions. But, though she was shrewd and likable, there were times when only her good nature saved her from assault. For Tilly Parsons refused to learn how to spell. She had a habit of suddenly flinging open the door, bursting in, and on the same instant hurling out a question as to how you spelled something, which made William Cartwright leap half-way to the ceiling.

"For the love of God, Tilly, why don't you get a dictionary? Are you too lazy to work a dictionary?"

"I'm sorry, Bill. Are you busy?"

"Yes."

"Well, I won't do it again. How do you spell exaggerated?"

She would then sit down on his desk, pushing the papers to one side, and talk shop until escorted out by main force.

But it could not be denied that she had taught Monica Stanton a good deal. Tilly, tough as nails, had taken to Monica. Cartwright, himself a hard and conscientious workman, had to admit that Tilly knew every trick of a dull trade. And Monica—

The typewriters ticked and tapped behind closed doors in the other offices. Cartwright, noting that it was time either to draw the blackout curtains or shut up shop and go home, was too baffled and depressed to do either. It was one of the moods we all know. Monica—

From the noise of the typewriter, he could visualize

Monica bent over it. The wide-spaced eyes would be fixed tensely on the paper in the carriage; the short, full upper lip would be out, a cigarette in one corner of the mouth in full sophisticated style, except when the smoke got into her eye; her shoe would rapidly tap the floor; and she would fly at it again, with many erasures. The first time he had ever set eyes on her, he knew he liked her. Within an hour of that encounter, he had a wild and disturbing idea that he was falling for her. Within forty-eight hours—

It was bad. It made him feel like a schoolboy. It brought palpitations of the chest and wrought strange phenomena in the nervous system. It—

With a crash audible at the other end of the building, the white door to the corridor flew open.

"Bill," said Tilly Parsons, bursting out at him, "how do you spell exaggerated?"

3

Tilly had entered by the corridor door so as not to disturb Monica. Her lipstick was again on sideways. On her left hand, flopped across the knob of the door, she wore a big gold wedding ring; she had a husband in the States, whom nobody had ever seen, but her views on marriage would have been considered cynical even by the early Fathers of the Church.

"What ho, what ho!" lamented Tilly, in her hoarse cigarette voice. She smiled. "Did I make you jump?"

He conquered the hot-and-cold wave which had swept up from his chest to his head, and made it swim.

"No."

"Sure I didn't, honey?"

"No. But you are gradually driving me to the loony-bin. I informed you last week that exaggerated was spelled e-x-a-g-g-e-r-a-t-e-d. Unless the authorities have got together and done something about it in the meantime, it is still spelled like that."

Tilly laughed, a harsh but not unpleasant sound.

"That's what I thought you said. — Busy?"

"No."

Tilly looked at him shrewdly, the half-smile still on her broad face. Then she plumped across to the desk. Carefully sweeping a heap of manuscript-sheets off on the floor, she hauled herself up and sat down on the desk, diving into her pocket after cigarettes.

"Mind if I sit down?"

"Not at all."

"Have a Chester?"

"No, thanks. This is my tipple." He felt that his mood called for heroic measures. Running his eye over the row of pipes, he picked up the death's-head meerschaum in loving fingers, and filled it out of an earthen jar.

"Alas, poor Yorick," said Tilly, watching him. "Judas, what a sight for sore eyes *that* is."

"This, Tilly, is a werry handsome pipe. Tilly, how would you like to be kissed by someone with a beard?"

"Are you propositioning me?" asked Tilly, lighting the cigarette before he could strike a match for her.

"Not exactly. That is to say, you are the light of my life, of course—"

"Horse feathers," said Tilly, with definiteness. But she did not say it in the tone usually employed in these exchanges. She spoke in a serious, rather absent-minded voice. Ever since she had come in, he had got the impression that there was something weighty on her mind, and that she wriggled under it. She put one hand, with a swashbuckling gesture, on her hip; the red end of the cigarette glowed in the darkening room.

"What's the matter, honey?" she asked, in a different voice. "Got the whips and jingles?"

"Yes."

Tilly bent forward. She assumed a look of secrecy and mysteriousness so intense that he instinctively looked round, to make sure they were not overheard. She raised her eyebrows and kept her eyes fixed on him. Stealthily she pointed to the door of Monica's room.

"Is it—?"

"Yes."

Tilly hesitated. Her air of mysteriousness increased. Sliding off the desk, she tiptoed over to the closed door of Monica's room and listened. She was answered by a ragged rattle of typewriter keys, which appeared to satisfy her. She tiptoed back, bent over him, and glared at him. The tone she employed was unnerving: for unimportant information, her voice kept its normal hoarseness; for important information, she suddenly lowered it to a whisper, aided by expressive grimaces.

"Listen," she said. "You're one of these educated guys, aren't you?"

"I suppose you could call it that."

"Have you got any money?"

"Some. I do fairly well."

"And you've fallen for her?" Here Tilly's voice became a hacking whisper, aided by a gesture towards the door. "Honest, I mean, and strike you dead? No fooling?"

"Honest, and strike me dead."

"I don't think you're a fake," said Tilly, eyeing him. "Christ, how I hate fakes!" There was real passion in her voice. "I think you're all right. And I'm going to tell you two things about that girl. The first is: she's fallen for you too."

The light had faded so that it was barely possible to make out Tilly's grimace of emphasis. Evidently seeing the incredulity which struck him dumb, and turned the wits to water in his head, Tilly raised her hand as though taking an oath and concluded by crossing her heart.

"But —"

"*Sh-h!*" hissed Tilly.

"Yes, but —"

"I ought to know, oughtn't I?" asked Tilly. She could not hiss this, there being no sibilant in it, but she gave the impression of doing so. "I bunk in the same house as her, don't I? Her room's next to mine, isn't it? I see her most of the day and half the night, don't I?"

"Yes, but —"

"*Sh-h!*"

As a conspirator, Tilly would have been recognized anywhere on the screen. She put her finger to her lips, and pointed to the door. There was, indeed, a suspicious silence inside; as of someone listening. So

Tilly spoke in a loud, hearty, careless voice.

"Aren't you going to draw the curtains? Shame on you, Bill! Be a sport and draw the curtains. What'll the Air Raid Warden think?"

He moved obediently over to the nearest window, which was open. At the moment nothing could have interested him less than the opinions of the Air Raid Warden.

Outside, the low bank of the lake stretched to a point within twenty feet of the windows. In twilight the lake looked whitish and vast, contrasting with the yellow and black shapes of tattered trees beyond. The last gleams of daylight touched the far edge of it, making silhouettes of the figures of two men who were standing on the nearer bank, and whose voices rose faintly.

One was a short fat man with a cigar, the other a tall spectacled young man with an ultra-refined accent.

"Lookit," said the fat man. "This last big scene at the end of the Battle of Waterloo."

"Yes, Mr. Aaronson?"

"This big scene," amplified the fat man, "where the Duke of Wellington dies in the moment of victory."

"But the Duke of Wellington did not die in the moment of victory, Mr. Aaronson."

"He didn't?"

"No, Mr. Aaronson. The Battle of Waterloo was fought in the year 1815. The Duke of Wellington did not die until the year 1852."

There was a loud noise as the fat man smote his forehead.

"Jeez, you're right. You're absolutely and positively right. I remember now. I was thinking of the other guy. You know. The one with his hat on in front instead of sideways."

"You mean Lord Nelson, Mr. Aaronson?"

"That's it. Nelson. He died in the moment of victory, didn't he?"

"Yes, Mr. Aaronson."

"I thought so. Well, then, we got to change the picture."

"Yes, Mr. Aaronson."

"And I got a better idea than that. Boy, is this a knockout! Lookit. He don't die. But they *think* he's going to die, see? He's lying on his camp-bed, and the audience thinks he's going to kick the bucket for sure. And then (here's the big kick, see?) his life is saved by an American surgeon."

"But, Mr. Aaronson—"

"I've been thinking about this picture anyway. It's too English, that's what's the trouble with it. We got to remember Oshkosh and Peoria."

"Do I understand, Mr. Aaronson, that you would like to have the Duke of Wellington's life saved by an American surgeon from Oshkosh or Peoria?"

"No, no, no, you don't get the idea at all. It's this way. The Duchess of Richmond—"

William Cartwright, though as a rule he relished these conversations, paid little attention to this one. It is doubtful if he even heard it. Drawing deeply on the skull-pipe, he closed the window. He drew the air-raid curtains, which were of thin black material having little protection against light unless backed by the heavy regular curtains, and drew these as well. He sealed up the other window. Then he groped back to the desk and switched on the light.

Tilly was now revealed as a pleasant, tubby little woman with patently peroxided hair. Though a nagging of worry remained in her eyes, a great load seemed to have gone off her mind.

"Don't look so dazed," she complained, drawing at her cigarette. "You can take it from me, Bill. It's a fact."

"It is a fact," said Cartwright, "of which I am not altogether persuaded. How do you know this? Did she tell you?"

"*Sh-h!* No! She'd kill me if she thought I was talking about it. But that's how she feels. That is, except when she gets a letter from her family, and then she tries to think she hates your innards."

"Why? Are her family against me?"

"No; that's the trouble: they're for you. You know them, don't you?"

Cartwright stared at her.

"To the best of my knowledge, I never set eyes on any member of her family in my life."

"Well, you must have met them somewhere. Her old man's a parson; and he wouldn't lie, would he?" Tilly sighed, and then looked sour. "Anyway, I wish you luck. Monica's a nice kid. She's what I'd call a ginch; sweet voice, and big eyes, and sort of hesitate-and-wonder manner. If I was a man, that's the sort of thing I'd go for."

Cartwright sat down, the pipe clamped between his teeth. He put his elbows on the desk, and ruffled the hair at his temples. As a matter of philosophical fact he was merely confused; his feeling was the one for which Bovril is so notoriously recommended. At any other time he would have been astounded at the platitudes he heard himself uttering.

"It's a funny world, Tilly."

"It sure is. But what are you going to *do?*"

"Do!"

"Yes, do! I know what you ought to do, Bill Cartwright. You take my tip: you just walk straight in there now, and grab her."

"So?"

"Certainly. Give her the old cave-man stuff." Tilly's expression grew very earnest; she opened her eyes wide. "But I'm warning you, honey. There's one thing you've got to do first. Take off that spinach."

"What spinach?"

"*That.* Those whiskers," hissed Tilly, with a touch of impatience. She blew out smoke with a broad nervous movement of her shoulders, and stubbed out the cigarette in the ashtray. "Otherwise she'd only wallop you. What's the matter with you, anyway? Do you think any woman wants to be grabbed by the inside of a mattress?"

Inspiration came to Tilly. Her eye was forever applied to the range-finder of a camera; she saw all life as box-office. She bent closer.

"*Sh-h!* Listen. I've got a pair of nail-scissors in my room. I'll sneak down there, and get 'em, and sneak back. You cut the beard close with the scissors, and shave it off in the cloakroom there. I know you've got shaving things here, because you spent the night on that sofa when you forgot your flashlight. Off comes the spinach. And then you're set. You just walk in the other room, and—" She made a triumphant gesture toward the door.

"You want me to—"

"*Sh-h!*"

"All right, all right. But it's getting late, Tilly. She'll be leaving."

"No, she won't. She's all full of inspiration and orneriness. She's got a bottle of milk and some crackers in there, and she says she's going to work half the night. Besides—" Tilly stopped abruptly. She studied him. Her eyes opened still wider. "Bill Cartwright, where's the old fight? What's wrong with you? You haven't used a six-syllable word since I've been in here. Great suffering catfish, I believe you're *afraid*."

"*Sh-h!*" hissed Cartwright.

"Well, aren't you?"

"Certainly not," he returned, telling as much truth as he knew. "If you will kindly close those delicate lips of yours for five seconds, and allow me to get a word in edgeways, I will endeavor to explain my position in the matter."

"Now that's more like you," cried Tilly admiringly. "Go on, honey. I'm listening."

He put down his pipe in the ashtray. "In the first place, Tilly, let's establish something. I'm not the one who's uneasy: that is, not much. You are."

"I am?"

"Yes. I want to know the reason for your sudden plunge into match-making. Not that I'm not grateful. But why? To be specific, what's on your mind?"

"All right; you asked for it," breathed Tilly. She sat for a time silent under the light of the hanging lamp above the desk; which showed her foreshortened, as though she were squeezed together like a concertina.

Her plump hands were tightly clenched, the flesh shiny and sagging across the backs of the hands; and the big wedding-ring glittered as she twisted it.

"Because Monica's a nice kid," she said. "And if you don't take care of her, nobody will. She's scared, Bill."

"Scared? Why?"

"Because I've got an idea," answered Tilly, looking him in the eyes, "that somebody is going to try to kill her, and maybe tonight."

VII

It had returned again.

So he was a cashiered prophet, was he? A demoted calamity-howler at whom both Hackett and Fisk now grinned? Back to him in one rush came all the beliefs whose importance had been swept aside under the advent of war: the evidence at which nobody would look and the theories to which nobody would listen. He remembered an interview he had had with Chief Inspector Humphrey Masters in London a fortnight ago. He remembered how Masters had assured him, blandly, that it was probably all a practical joke; that it would be criminal to bother Sir Henry Merrivale with it, at a time like this; and that he would only clog the already overburdened post office by writing.

Yet in the lower drawer of that desk he had his evidence.

"How do you know that?" he demanded. His voice sounded shatteringly loud in the white-painted room.

"Sh-h! That's what I think, anyway."

"But how do you know it?"

"Anonymous letters. She's had two of them in the

past week. Maybe more, for all I know."

Cartwright took Tilly firmly by the arm. He led her across the room and into the cloakroom, which was no more than a biggish compartment built into one corner of the office. It had a small window, which escaped the necessity for war-time curtains by being covered with black paint. The place was a mess, since he, like Tilly, brewed coffee to write on; but this was not a time to apologize for the house-keeping. He closed the door and switched on the light.

"Now, then," he said, "stop whispering and tell me what you mean."

Tilly herself seemed scared by the earnestness of his manner. But her jaw was defiant.

"Read that," she said. "Go on; read it."

It was a folded half sheet of notepaper, of the pinkish sort you can buy at Woolworth's, which she took out of her coat pocket and flung at him. On it there were a few lines of writing in dark-blue ink.

All right, Bright-eyes. I'm not through with you yet. Your Dad and your Aunt Flossie are going to get a pleasant surprise soon. The vitriol was a washout; but I've got another little treat saved up for you. This time you won't be able to jump back.

It was not only that the writing itself seemed to breathe malice in every line. But he only saw what he expected to see.

In his mind was a vivid memory of a blackboard by the door of sound stage number three, with words

112

scrawled across it in chalk. A photograph of those words lay in the lower drawer of his desk now. And, so far as he could tell without comparison, the handwriting of this letter was the same as the handwriting on the blackboard.

William Cartwright felt slightly sick.

"You say she's been getting letters like this?"

"Two, anyway. One came this morning."

"What did it say?"

"I don't know, honey. She didn't show me any of 'em."

"Then how did you get this?"

"I stole it," returned Tilly, without embarassment. "I thought it was time somebody did."

"You stole it?"

"Out of her bedroom. I couldn't get a look at the letter she got today, except for just a flash. It said something about 'tonight.' That didn't look so good to little Tilly."

It was still difficult to realize. "You say she's been getting these letters for a week and still hasn't said anything about it to anybody?"

"Of course not," growled Tilly, angrily taking another cigarette out of her pocket and lighting it. A bit of tobacco adhered to her broad-painted mouth; she dislodged it with a scarlet finger-nail, still angrily. "The girl's movie-crazy. She's dippy about all this. I've been in this game for eighteen years; and I've seen it happen time and time again. You think it's dull. I think it's good bread-and-butter. But *she* thinks it's wonderful."

"Yes."

"She's afraid they'll send her away, and not let her

113

work in sight of all the lovely sets. Look, Bill. I've been hearing rumors. There was something that happened two or three weeks ago—something about vitriol?—"

She paused.

"Yes," he said.

Tilly's mouth was grim. But the shadow of both anger and fright lurked about her wizened eyelids.

"That's a kid for you. That's a kid all over. She says ha-ha to these letters. She's much more afraid Tommy Hackett will find out about the letters, and think she's in danger, and chase her away for her own good. Judas, I give up. It's some situation. What with a maniac hanging around the place, and never going to bed without wondering whether the air-raid siren's going to go—"

This was the sort of talk which must be stopped.

"Now, Tilly," he said wearily, "don't you start talking like that. You're in absolutely no danger. Don't you know that?"

"Oh, yes, I know. I know England's got the air force. I know that the minute somebody takes a crack at London, they'll go over the next night and blow Berlin to glory. But that's no consolation to *me*. Judas, will I be glad when this job's over and I can get back to the States."

He shrugged his shoulders.

"Well, Tilly, it's your privilege to go now, if you want to."

"Look," said Tilly. She put one flabby hand on the edge of the table that held the gas-ring, and grinned at him. "What I want is a cocktail and some dinner, that's all. If the English can think these blackouts are no trouble at all, I can take it too. You're a funny crowd: the more trouble they put you to, the more jokes you make about it. It's just this waiting—like what that kid in there must be doing."

She took a handkerchief out of the inexhaustible pocket of her flannel suit, and blew her nose.

"But, you see, the kid won't tell me anything! I was there when she got the first letter. I said, "Is anything wrong, dearie?" and she just said, 'No.' Like that."

"How does she get these letters? Through the post?"

"No. By hand."

Cartwright stared at her. "By hand? At the Merefield Country Club?"

"At the Merefield Country Club. They get pushed under the door. At least, two of 'em were."

"Who else lives at the Club besides you two?"

"The whole dam' shoot. Tommy Hackett and Howard Fisk and Dick Conyers and Bella Darless and—no, Mr. and Mrs. Gagern have got a cottage like you, you plutocrat. There's another pair of love-birds for you. But anybody's got access to the Club." Tilly finished blowing her nose; she winked her eyes, returned the handkerchief to her pocket, and drew deeply at the cigarette. "Anyway, that's my story. It's no business of mine. But I don't want to see that kid wind up behind the eightball if I can help it. Now then, Bill Cartwright, are you going to go and shave off that spinach and go straight in and have it out with Monica, or aren't you?"

He snorted.

"You can bet I am, Tilly. Though never mind the spinach. That can wait for more important—"

"Oh, you dope!" shouted Tilly, transformed. She reached up and laid hold of his shoulders. "Can't you get it through your thick head how important that is?"

Cartwright set himself, and made a broad oratorical gesture which knocked to the floor, with a ringing clatter, a pan half full of coffee grounds.

"My dear Tilly, if my beard is such an offense in the sight of heaven, very well. Off it comes. There is my hand on it. But just at the moment I have some comparisons to make. I think I know who this malicious swine is"—he held up the letter—"but for the life of me I can't tell *why*. There is a certain person I have been keeping an eye on (with some care, Tilly) for the past three weeks. And in my desk out there . . ."

"Hello!" called Monica's voice, from the other room. There was a noise of quick footsteps. "Hello! Where have you two hidden yourselves?"

2

She was standing in the middle of Cartwright's office when a guilty-looking pair tumbled out of the cloakroom.

He wondered if she had overheard. For the atmosphere had changed. Monica's manner was very casual, though there was color under her eyes. She wore blue slacks and a blue jumper, and had a light coat drawn across her shoulders. Her long, soft hair was somewhat disarranged; a stain of typewriter ink on her fingers had been partly transferred to her cheek.

"Oh, there you are," she said without inflection. "Tilly, what does it mean when it says the camera 'dollies back and pans out'?"

"What's that, dearie?"

"What does it mean when it says the camera 'dollies back and pans out'?"

Tilly explained, though Cartwright was certain he had answered the same question from her less than a fortnight ago.

"Oh," said Monica.

She put her finger on Cartwright's desk, and twisted it there. She hesitated. The gray-blue eyes, widely spaced on either side of the short nose, sent an oblique glance between Tilly and Cartwright.

She hesitated again.

"I've blacked out your windows," she went on, as though from a hollow silence. "I mean in your room, Tilly."

"Thanks, dearie."

"Please, can't you do it yourself more often? I—I mean, see that they're *properly* blacked out? It always makes me jump when that man comes bawling under the windows, at the same eternal time every night, shouting 'lights' at us."

"I'll attend to it, honey."

Monica stopped twisting her finger on the table.

"What were you two whispering about?" she asked.

"Nothing, dearie. Nothing at all!"

"What's the good of talking like that?" Cartwright suddenly demanded. He took the sheet of pink notepaper out of his pocket and put it on the table by her finger. "We were talking about you, Monica. We've got to have this out. We—"

He stopped just as suddenly, while the emotional temperature of the room shot up.

The door to the corridor opened, catching them all in that same mid-flight of emotion. There appeared in the doorway the beaming and benevolent face of Howard Fisk.

"Evening, everybody," he whispered, rapping on the inside of the door to emphasize his entrance. "What sort of hours do you people keep down here, anyway?"

Monica had checked herself, her lips half open and her fists clenched. Tilly Parsons coughed loudly. Only Fisk himself seemed unconscious of an atmosphere. He lumbered under the doorway, exuding an odor of tweeds, an old hat on the back of his head.

"You've been living like hermits down here," he complained; and his pince-nez twinkled. "Nobody's seen the face of any of you for a week. Hello, Tilly. Hello, Monica. Hello, Bill. Now see here, all of you. I'm here to take Monica out to dinner."

Monica turned her head sideways.

"Dinner?" she echoed.

"Yes, dinner. I've barked my shins and broken my neck to get down from the main building without a torch; and I won't take no for an answer. Up there I've got a golden chariot, with petrol in it for probably the last time. We're going into town and splurge at the Dorchester; and we're not going to dress for it either. Hop to it, young lady."

"But, Mr. Fisk—"

"The name is Howard."

"I can't," said Monica. "I'd love to, but I can't."

"Just tell me why not?"

Monica suddenly seemed to be conscious of the ink stains on her fingers.

"Because I can't, honestly. This is Monday. You and Mr. Hackett are coming in on Wednesday to look at the completed script; and I'm 'way behind. It's the detective part." Her eyes slid towards Cartwright.

"Oh, tut, tut! Hackett doesn't pay you to be as conscientious as that. It'll keep for one night. Come on!"

"I can't. I'm terribly sorry."

Howard Fisk hesitated.

"I don't know what's the matter," he complained, "that I can never get you to go out with me. What about you, Tilly?"

"Sorry; got a date already."

The director drew a deep breath. His air was disconsolate. He turned to Monica. "Well, then, if you insist on being businesslike, I may as well not waste a trip down here. I wonder if I could see you alone for five minutes? It's Sequence B, that underground business. Do you think we could clean it up now?"

"No!" said Tilly Parsons.

It was involuntary. It burst from her in her harshest croak; it jabbed the nerves like a needle under a tooth; it startled them all, but notably Fisk, who turned in obvious surprise.

"Eh?" he said.

In a fraction of a second Tilly was herself again. She laughed, dropped her cigarette on the linoleum floor and trod it out.

"What a woman," she mocked herself. "Just a

119

touch of hangover, that's all. I was out with the boys last night, and I can still feel the floor rock in that pub. Pay no attention."

"Of course," said Monica. "Please come into my office, Mr. Fisk."

She held open the door.

Past her shoulder and through the door, they could see one wall of the little office. Monica was as tidy in her habits as she was untidy of thought. On a side table against the wall were neatly ranged a little line of reference books, an untouched ream of paper with two erasers, and her gas mask in a leather container. Over it on the wall hung a framed photograph of Canon Stanton. This last had caused some ribaldry among those who visited the room; but to Cartwright—his senses and his imagination strung up—it brought a domestic touch, a feeling of honest things in a house of make-believe.

The door closed behind the other two; and Tilly glowered at him.

"Well," she said grimly, "you sure blurted it out. About the letters. What are you going to do now?"

"Wait until Howard goes, and blurt out the rest of it."

"I thought so," said Tilly. "In that case, there's something I've got to get. I'll be back in a minute, so hold everything."

He did not hear her go. The image of words, written on a pinkish sheet of paper out of a sixpenny box, rose in his mind with too much unpleasant suggestion.

All right, Bright-eyes. I'm not through with you yet.

120

He had thought there might be something on the way, and he was right.

Your Dad and your Aunt Flossie are going to get a pleasant surprise soon.

He went back to his desk. Taking a bunch of keys out of his pocket, he unlocked the lower drawer. It contained a typewritten resumé of what had happened in the soundstage on the afternoon of August 23, with accounts of where people said they were at various times. It contained a certain empty bottle. It contained a big photograph of the writing on the blackboard.

He put the piece of pink notepaper side by side with the photograph, and took a glass to them.

It checked. There could be no doubt whatever about that. The handwriting on the blackboard was the same as the handwriting on the letter.

The vitriol was a washout; but I've got another little treat saved up for you.

There was not a sound in the whole building except the faint drone of voices from Monica's room. The lamp, in its dark conical shade, shed a bright light on the metal fittings of the typewriter. William Cartwright put down the magnifying glass. He stared at the keys of the typewriter. He picked up a pipe at random, and chewed on the stem of it.

Presently he pulled open the upper drawer of his desk. That drawer contained, in addition to paper and envelopes, some rough notes for a new story; they concerned a certain virulent poison, the way to procure that poison, and a diabolically ingenious way of administering it. If his mind had not been occupied with other matters, he would have had the sense to lock those notes into the lower drawer.

But he never thought of it. He rolled a sheet of notepaper into the carriage of the typewriter, dated it, and wrote rapidly.

Sir Henry Merrivale,
The War Office,
Whitehall, S.W.1.

Dear Sir:

I am a friend of Chief Inspector Masters: I will not waste your time with further introductions.

We need help and we need advice. If I were not sure that the matter concerned your department, Military Intelligence, I should not bother you. Just under three weeks ago, we had a near-murder here. I think I can tell you who is responsible —

"Here you are, honey," said Tilly Parsons, appearing suddenly at his elbow. She banged down on the desk not only a pair of nail-scissors, but a pair of long-bladed paper-cutting scissors as well.

"Go away," said William Cartwright wildly.

"Come on, honey," said Tilly, with sternness. "Take off that spinach. If the nail-scissors won't do to start it, the big ones will."

To devil a man engaged in literary composition is one of the primary mistakes which can be made by the daughters of Eve.

"For the love of Satan and all the thrice-accursed

hosts," howled Cartwright, starting up, "will you get out of here and stay out? Aroint ye. Scram. Can't you think of anything but beards? Are you mad on the subject of beards? I am trying to devote serious attention to a serious question, and all you can think of—"

Tilly extended the long-bladed scissors.

"For the last time, laddie, will you take off that spinach?"

"For the last time, woman, I will not."

Tilly was a woman of action. She hesitated no longer. The big scissors were extended, and she handled them with the precision of a swordsman. With one deft chop she cut off not only the end of Cartwright's beard, but very nearly the end of his chin as well.

"Now will you take 'em off?" she asked.

Some weeks ago, Monica Stanton had been merely stupefied—past speech—by a lack of tact which seemed to her to be beyond human comprehension. It was now William Cartwright's turn to feel the same emotion. He merely stared at Tilly. He saw red. A more easy-going man did not exist, but for a moment he quite seriously considered picking up the chair and hitting her over the head with it.

Cold rage ensued. He took the scissors from Tilly, who was really alarmed now. He walked quietly into the cloakroom. He switched on the light. He ran hot water into the wash-bowl. He arranged shaving-tackle on the glass shelf above it.

In ten minutes the beard was no more.

"Judas!" said Tilly wonderingly. "I wouldn't have believed it could make so much improvement. It makes you look ten years younger. It makes you not bad-looking, even. Are you going to take off the mustache too?"

He looked at her for a second, and then turned back to the wash-bowl.

"Now, you whey-faced witch," shouted the impolite Mr. Cartwright, turning round in conclusion and hurling the towel over the gas-ring, "is there anything further I can do for you? Would you care to see me have my appendix out? Would it amuse you if I shaved my head and painted it green? If so—"

"Don't get sore, honey. You've cut your chin. Stick some stuff on it."

"Good night, everybody!" cried Howard Fisk's voice, distantly. "If you people don't want your dinner, I do. Good night."

A door slammed.

"Now's your chance," hissed Tilly. "Go on in and do your stuff. I'll be waiting in my room. You look fine. You don't look like Mr. William Cartwright. You look like Bill."

It seemed to the newly christened Bill, as she impelled him across the room, that both he and Tilly were behaving in a somewhat ridiculous manner.

If he could not put his finger on the way in which they were behaving foolishly, he at least knew why. Tilly behaved so because she was nervous. He behaved so because he was in love with Monica Stanton, and didn't give a damn.

Yet, as he lifted his hand to knock, he experienced certain qualms. His face, still tingling, felt very bare. Hitherto that beard had been his defence in encounters; he had marched, so to speak, behind brush, like

Macduff against Dunsinane. The beard had given him (he thought) an appearance of mature years and sober wisdom. That was why he had grown it. His ideal, so far as appearances went, would have been to attain the age of about forty-five and stay there.

He knocked.

"Monica—"

She did not turn around.

She was sitting at her desk in the middle of the room, with her back to him, bent over the typewriter. The light, brilliant and unshaded, showed the side of a flushed face. He felt that she was angry. What he did not know was that the girl was very near to tears.

"Monica—"

"So it was you," she said, still without turning round, "who stole it."

His mind, momentarily diverted, was brought up against this with a bump. A cloud of cigarette smoke hung in the room.

"Stole what?"

"You know what. That letter."

Comprehension returned; and, with it, determination. "Monica, look here. You've got to listen to me. I didn't steal your letter, but I ruddy well would have if I'd known anything about it. I want to help you. Curse it all, I lo—"

"Oh!" gasped Monica.

This was where she turned round.

It was an all-too-natural reaction: she laughed in his face. She leaned back, kicking her heels on the floor, and whooped with mirth until the tears came.

After a frozen silence he looked round. He saw the flushed, lovely face distorted with merriment; he saw

125

even the photograph of Canon Stanton smiling indulgently at him from the wall. But something can here be said to the credit of the new Bill Cartwright. He did not, as his first impulse was, turn around and walk out of the room. He advanced to the desk.

"Then that is settled," he said grimly. "If you insist, it is funny. I will agree, without a struggle, that it is the funniest spectacle since the hanging of Larry O'Halloran. We will sit right down here and split our sides over it. But you are going to listen to me just the same. I am not going to have you go about any longer in danger of being attacked by that swine. I think too much of you for that. Here is the plain fact. I lo—"

"Old Building! Lights!"

It blattered out, on dead silence, in the same familiar way. It made them both jump and turn towards the windows. The usual guardian was making his rounds outside the windows at the usual time.

"Old Building! Lights showing!" bawled the voice.

Monica was looking at Bill Cartwright.

"Wh-what did you say?" she asked.

"Miss Stanton! Middle room! Lights!"

"Wh-what did you say?"

"Miss Stanton! Middle room! Top of blackout curtain! Chink showing!"

An invisible hand hammered on the glass of one window.

"Miss Stanton! Lights!"

Monica went to the window—it would be fair to say that she flew at it—as the voice faded away. She pulled back the heavy inner curtains to their full width, and raised her hands to the black curtains

126

underneath.

Bill watched her go. In an abstract way he saw the details of the room, lit by a naked glare of electricity. He saw the blackout curtains, smoothly drawn together without a chink down their length. He saw Monica squarely facing the oblong of the window, her arms raised and her fingers fumbling with the top of the curtain-rod. He saw her shadow, blacker still on the black sateen. He saw—

This time you won't be able to jump back.

It was the wrong voice.

"Down!" he yelled. *"Down!"*

He was just too late. The crash of the explosion shook the window-pane as he ran for her.

The bullet had been fired at Monica's face. It drilled a hole in the window-pane without shattering the glass, and left another hole in the curtain at about the height of her ear.

3

When he considered it afterwards, it always seemed that these things took a very long time, though in point of fact it was a matter of seconds.

Monica, still at the window, made a gesture. There was a very faint reddish patch on her left temple by the edge of her hair, like a slight abrasion before it begins to bleed. That was where the bullet had grazed, before it smashed the picture of Canon Stanton against the opposite wall.

The door communicating with Tilly Parson's room

was flung open. Tilly stood in the doorway, her jaw-muscles loose and the lipstick standing out vividly against her face. Behind her, the office was a drift of crumpled papers; a cup of coffee steamed on Tilly's desk, and a cigarette smoldered on the edge of the standing ashtray.

Her voice was so hoarse as to be barely audible.

"Was it — ?" she said.

"I'm quite all right," said Monica, none too steadily. "He missed again."

"You're hurt dearie. I can see it! You're—"

"I'm quite all right," said Monica.

But she went over and sat down on the sofa. Bill Cartwright managed to speak.

"Got a torch, Tilly?"

Tilly turned blazing eyes. "You going out after the so-and-so?"

"Yes. He's got to run along the edge of the lake. He can't get across it. Give me a torch, quick! I might still be in time."

Tilly ran to her office and waddled back with a flashlight.

"I know that voice," she said. "I've heard that voice: I mean the so-and-so who pretended to be the groundkeeper yelling 'lights.' Where have I heard that voice? Where—"

But Bill was already out of the room, the door banging. For a time there was no sound in Monica's office except that of hard breathing. Tilly took out a handkerchief and wiped her eyes; she seemed as much excited as moved.

"Let me bathe your head, honey. Come on! Let me put some stuff on your head."

"No. Not just for a minute, please."

"Would you like a little drink, honey?" wheedled Tilly. "I've got one, if you'd like it."

"Not for a minute."

Monica sat on the sofa, her hand shading her eyes. Then she got up and went over to the photograph of her father. Canon Stanton continued to smile. The bullet had smashed the glass, making a hole in the Canon's collar to bury itself in the wall behind; the picture hung sideways.

Taking down the picture, Monica looked at the splintered abrasion in the wall. She carried the broken picture over to her desk. Here, in the ordered neatness of things, she put it down beside a Victorian needlework box in red leather: a present from Miss Flossie Stanton, which Monica now kept full of cigarettes.

Tilly regarded her rather grimly.

"Are you going to give it up now, honey?"

"Give what up?"

"Are you going to get away from this place, like he wants you to?"

"I-I don't know. No, I'm not!"

"Easy, honey."

"I'm all right."

"Have a Chester," urged Tilly, dragging out the packet as though inspired. "English cigarettes are muck, dearie. I wouldn't smoke one on a bet. Dearie, look." She paused. "He didn't swipe your letter. I did."

"I thought so."

"Then why did you say—?"

"Oh, never mind."

"It was for your own good," said Tilly, "Honestly it was. He didn't know anything about it until tonight. I told him; I told him everything. You trust him. He thinks he knows who's been doing this: he's been watching somebody. Why do you want to be so uppish? I told him you'd fallen for him."

Monica gasped.

"You told him—"

"Ah, why deny it, dearie? It's true. You know it's true."

"It's not true!"

"It's as true as gospel. Why, you even talk about it in your sleep. I remember the other night. I thought I heard somebody muttering, and I got up and put my head in your room. And it was you. It was something about his being a Roman, or your being a Roman, or your both being a Roman; but anyway, honey, it was *something,* I can tell you."

Monica stared at her with widening eyes, and a widening flush which made her cheeks bright pink. She seemed to have difficulty in getting her breath.

"That settles it," she breathed, after a long pause. "I was trying to make up my mind, but that settles it. That beast!"

"But he didn't do anything, honey. Don't blame him just because he knows. Blame me. I told him. He didn't do anything except shave off his beard because he thought it would please you."

"I hope a lion bites him," said Monica. "If he comes anywhere near me, *I'll* bite him. I never want to have anything more to do with him as long as I live."

"Sh-h!" whispered Tilly, jerking up her head.

Both of them whirled round toward the window. Outside, clear on the night air, came what sounded like a view-halloo bellow from Bill Cartwright. A noise of running feet burst out, dodged, and grew more distant; there was a terrific splash from the lake, a thrashing, a triumphant howl from Cartwright, and more footsteps pounding away along the bank.

VIII

That was Monday night. On the afternoon of Wednesday, September 13, Bill Cartwright was entering the courtyard of the War Office.

He had not really expected a reply to the letter he had ultimately finished on Monday night and put into the eleven o'clock post. At least, he had not expected more than an acknowledgment of receipt. But an answer, on Wednesday morning, came with such promptness as to startle him and make him wonder.

The reply gave no information. It merely stated that if he would come to the enquiry-office of the War Office, entrance in Horseguards Avenue, if he would present this letter and ask for Captain Blake, the messenger would do the rest.

Meaning—?

Craftily, as he thought, he persuaded Monica to go with him to London.

"Like to come along to the War Office? After all, it concerns you."

"No, thank you. In any case, I've told you I would

rather you didn't trouble yourself about me."

"Just as you like. But it's an interesting sight in itself. The War Office, shrine of Military Intelligence! Generals and pukka sahibs. Decorations galore. Marble halls, and deep carpets. King's Messengers dashing away on secret missions to the East. In *Desire* you sent Captain Royce to the place a dozen times, and so I thought perhaps—"

"We-el," said Monica. . . .

But the journey to town, in a train which stopped to take a nap five or six times in fourteen miles, was not a conspicuous success. Monica sat primly in one corner of the carriage, and refused to talk about anything except detective stories. It appeared that in her three weeks at Pineham she had read hundreds of them. He himself had once been foolish enough to introduce the character of a clergyman into one of his books; and what Monica did with this was nobody's business. Judging by the number of ecclesiastical errors he had committed, it seemed to him that it was only by miracle he had escaped being burnt at the stake.

He could not make the girl out. At one time, just before that shot was fired through the window, he could have sworn he saw in her face something he wanted most to see there.

Then, suddenly, it wasn't there. Not only was it not there, but the current of cold air which surrounded her had attained Arctic dimensions.

But once in London, and on their way to the famous War Office, she thawed a little. The wine-like September air had its effect. The sky, September blue, was dotted with the silver shapes of the captive

133

balloons. Little had changed in war time, except for the sand-bags buttressing some buildings, and the gas-mask containers which most of the crowd carried slung over their shoulders: but these were carried with rather the air of people carrying lunch boxes, and had a look more of festivity than of war.

"Bill," said Monica, in the taxi from Marylebone Street station. It was the first time she had used his Christian name for two days.

"Yes?"

"We *are* going to see Sir Henry Merrivale, aren't we? The head of the whole Military-Intelligence Department?"

"We are."

Monica began to wriggle.

They got out of the taxi at a courtyard, enclosed on three sides by a massive gray building, and paved with uneven small stones which reminded Monica unpleasantly of the cobblestones of Eighteen-eighty-two. A number of cars were parked in the courtyard. They moved in the direction towards which people seemed to be going—a big door on the left.

Inside, in a big, dingy reception room, it was crowded. Here there were no signs whatever of marble halls or deep carpets. And there were no uniforms, except one or two with the red arm-bands of staff officers. Bill Cartwright elbowed his way through the crowd to a counter on the left, where a capable-looking messenger, with one arm and a walrus mustache, was attempting to deal with a hundred things at once.

"Yes, sir? Got an appointment?"

Bill held out the letter.

"You're all right, sir," the other assured him heartily. "Just sit down over there and fill out one of those white slips."

While Monica's mind conjured up magnificent images behind those darkish walls, Bill filled out the slip. All things balance themselves. Upon Bill Cartwright the War Office was working exactly the same effect as the film studio had worked upon Monica Stanton. His hand shook so much that he could barely fill out the particulars. Now that he was here, with an actual introduction to Sir Henry Merrivale, what might not happen? Mightn't they give him a job in Military Intelligence, even? This, the ultimate dream of his life, was so dazzling a prospect as to make him resolve never to be so logical or so compelling as during the forthcoming interview.

He returned the slip.

"That's all right, sir," said the messenger, conferring with some others. "Captain Blake, Room 171. But what's this about 'Miss Stanton'?"

"That's this lady. She's with me."

The messenger's thick eyebrows went up. Some swift telepathic instinct warned Bill that he was about to receive a terrific kick under the ear.

"But the lady can't go up with you, sir."

"She can't?"

"No, sir."

He caught Monica's eye. After this Monica began to look very steadily and thoughtfully at the ceiling.

"But why not? My business here concerns this lady. She's the most important witness I have. It was because of her that I was granted an interview at all. She—"

135

"Sorry, sir," returned the messenger, with finality. He drew a black line across the slip. "The letter says you and nobody else. Didn't you know that when you brought the lady here?"

"Monica, I swear I didn't know that!"

"Why, Bill, of course you didn't," laughed Monica, suddenly galvanized into patting his arm. "I quite understand. It's hardly my place here anyway, is it?"

"Look here: I won't be long. You don't mind waiting here for me?"

"No, of course not. Not a bit."

"You're sure?"

"Good heavens, of course not!"

(You villain. You low, mean, despicable, sneaking *hound*.)

"Look, Monica: you mean that, don't you? You'll stay here? You swear to me you won't go back to Pineham?"

"Why, Bill, whyever should you think of such a thing? Of course I'll wait. You run along and have a good time."

"This way, sir," interposed the messenger, patient but weary. "Keep that white slip. You'll want it to get out again."

Holding tightly to the brief-case he had brought with him, Bill was escorted away.

2

"Phoeey!" said Sir Henry Merrivale.

Bill Cartwright, from information he had received

at various times from Chief Inspector Masters was prepared for certain things. He knew that H.M.'s manner was seldom one of effusive cordiality. He did not expect to be greeted with a slap on the back, or with the polished politeness of most Government departments. He knew that the old man was apt to get into a bit of tear now and then.

But at the same time he was not prepared for the extraordinary, quiet malignancy of H.M.'s expression. H.M. sat back in a creaky swivel chair, twiddling his thumbs over his paunch. His big bald head shone against the light from a window. His spectacles were pulled down on his broad nose, and the corners of his mouth were drawn down almost to his chin. On his face was an expression which would not have been out of place in the Chamber of Horrors at Madame Tussaud's.

Bill had already seen adventure. Captain Blake was not to be found in room 171, nor in room 346. Bill and the messenger traversed long, broad, businesslike corridors paved with dingy tile. They went up several flights of a broad, low stone staircase built round a central shaft. They passed much old lumber stacked in the corridors: wooden filing cases, chairs, ancient tables. They finally found Captain Blake's new quarters in room 6-something, whose door bore a little card labelled *M.I.*

Here, in a big office which looked like a draughtsman's room, Captain Blake grinned and shook hands. He wore a staff officer's uniform, and seemed to be in charge of a number of men in street clothes, who sat or wrote at various big bare tables and did not appear to be engaged in anything very secret.

"This way," said Captain Blake, leading him through more offices. "Mind those cabinets. We're doing some reorganization here. Sir Henry has been moved from his old office, and he — er — doesn't like it much."

"You mean he's on the war-path?"

The other hesitated. "No, not exactly," he said, looking very hard at Bill. "Only I thought I'd warn you. And I'll give you another tip. Whatever you do, don't mention the House of Lords."

There was no time to inquire the reason for H.M.'s antipathy toward the House of Lords. Captain Blake opened the door of an untidy office, with two windows overlooking the courtyard; and behind a broad desk H.M. sat and twiddled his thumbs and glared at them.

"I been expectin' you," he said. "Sit down, son."

"Thank you, sir."

"Have a cigar?"

"Thank you; I'll stick to the pipe, if you don't mind."

Bill Cartwright, if necessary, was prepared to outstare the devil himself. But this was rather different. While he filled one of his favorite pipes (an atrocity to Monica Stanton), two fishy-looking eyes continued to regard him over the tops of spectacles.

"I got here," said the big bulk in the alpaca coat, suddenly coming to life and stirring papers on his desk, "I got here a very rummy letter from you. I also got what you call a transcript of evidence. Now looky here, son." His voice changed slightly. "What's on your mind, exactly?"

Bill drew a deep breath.

"What is on my mind," he said, "is murder. At Pineham in the past three weeks we have had two attempted murders: one a piece of brutality so senseless that it sounds like the work of a maniac, and both directed against the same person. A girl named Monica Stanton."

"Uh-huh. Well?"

"This girl hasn't an enemy in the world. There seems to be no earthly reason why anybody should want to kill her. I want you to find out why, and to get the proof that will put this swine where he belongs. *I* can't get the proof. He is either phenomenally brilliant or phenomenally lucky. He openly leaves his handwriting on a blackboard, and on two letters—and yet I can't trace it to him. He openly shouts out words outside a window—and yet none of us can identify his voice. And this is all the worse because I am practically certain I know who the person is."

"Uh-huh. Who do you think it is?"

"A fellow by the name of Kurt von Gagern."

"Uh-huh. Reasons?"

"But, sir, I wrote you—"

"H'mf, yes. But never you mind that, son. Just tell me your reasons."

It was his chance.

"If I have the floor, then, I'd like to go back to the first incident that happened, exactly three weeks ago today. They were shooting a scene from a film called *Spies at Sea,* whose background was a bedroom cabin aboard a luxury liner. Howard Fisk (apparently by accident) knocked over the water bottle on the bedside table, and it was found to be full of sulphuric acid. Now that set was reproduced, it was said, from photographs of the German liner *Brünhilde;* but it was arranged and supervised by Gagern, who is famous for the realism of his details. . . . Sir Henry, did you ever travel aboard an Atlantic liner?"

"Sure, son. Well?"

"Well," said Bill Cartwright, "did you ever in your experience see a *glass* water bottle on a bedside table?"

After a pause he went on:

"I don't think you did. In luxury cabins, or any first-class cabins, there are only two types of water bottle. One is of very heavy glass; it is carefully placed, so that it can't fall over, in a rack above the wash-basin. The only other type of bottle you find is a thermos, with a heavy bakelite or chromium cover, which contains iced drinking water. The reason is patent. To put an ordinary glass water bottle — such as you or I might have in our homes — on the bedside table in a liner's cabin, would be plain lunacy. It would go over smash with the first roll of the ship.

"No steamship company would do that. No steamship company has ever done it. Gagern, who says he has crossed the Atlantic umpteen times, must have known that. Even if he didn't, there were the photographs of the *Brünhilde* to show him. No. I maintain that he put it there deliberately, on a table where it could be knocked over; and he deliberately saw to it that it *was* knocked over.

"Read what Howard Fisk has to say about that! Howard says, 'Gagern and I were talking, and I was walking backward, and he said, "Look out!" I bumped into that little table by the bed,' — and so on.

Gagern again, you see.

"Now, Howard Fisk's clumsiness is notorious. If I wanted to engage him in a conversation, crowding him backward so that he was certain to bump into something and upset it with his fifteen-stone weight, I will offer a small bet that I could do this without Howard or anybody else ever suspecting it was done deliberately. That, sir, is what happened. Gagern was the vitriol merchant. Which is the very devil of it. I will swear to my dying day he did it. But for the life of me I can't think why he did it."

3

He paused, and drew at a pipe that had gone out. Now Bill Cartwright at the War Office, like Monica Stanton at the film studio, suffered from being impressed so much that he barely noticed external things. He was talking his head off, before his audience should interrupt him. And he felt that he was talking well. If ever in his life he wanted to impress anybody, he wanted to impress these people.

Throughout this recital H.M. had not interrupted. Poker-players at the Diogenes Club have found any attempt to read H.M.'s face a high unprofitable proceeding.

"Well . . . now," he said, ruffling his hands across his big bald head. "That'd seem logical. Y'know, son, you remind me a bit of Masters. Got anything else?"

"Yes. The first attack on Monica Stanton."

"Well?"

"You have a resumé of her statement. You'll see what she says. A few minutes before the page-boy approached her, to tell her 'Mr. Hackett' wanted to see her on Eighteen-eighty-two, she was sitting near the oceanliner set and talking to Frances Fleur. They were getting on very well; they had just settled down to a good intimate chat, when all of a sudden F.F. seemed to notice something. She interrupted the talk, jumped up, excused herself hurriedly, and dashed off. The question was: why? . . . Do you know anything about Frances Fleur, by the way?"

"Ho ho," said H.M.

An expression of ghoulish pleasure went over his face. He rubbed his hands together. He treated Bill to what in anyone less eminently placed would have been called a lecherous leer, and chortled all over his stomach.

"I've seen her on the screen, son. Burn me, what a woman! I say, Ken." He turned to Captain Blake. "Do you remember the time we went to see her play Poppaea? And your wife carried on and called her names all the way through the show, and for the rest of the evening afterwards?"

"Well, sir," said Bill, "she's not Poppaea."

"No?"

"No. All F.F. asks from life, beyond a little admiration and attention, is just to sit down and take it easy. She's the director's prayer. She will sit for hours while you arrange lights or take stills; and all she asks is to talk during the meantime. She doesn't excuse herself for anybody. She doesn't jump up for anybody. She doesn't run for anybody."

He paused.

"That is — for anybody except one person. I mean her husband. He's the only person in the world who could make her do that. They've only been married a few months; I grant you it's a genuine love-match; and they do things in public that startle spectators and just stop short of actual business. She takes it casually; he takes it with kind of wolfish seriousness, as though he'd never seen a woman before.

"What Frances saw while she was talking to Monica (depend on it) was Gagern furiously beckoning her away. And then sending her somewhere on some tomfool errand. Otherwise, you see, Frances would have been talking to Monica until Doomsday. And Gagern had to have Monica alone. He had to have her alone so that she could be decoyed to the other set, and the acid poured down the speaking-tube into her face."

The words had an ugly ring; Bill Cartwright knew it.

H.M. spoke sharply. "Got any proof of that, son?"

"No, sir. And I'll tell you why.

"After the acid-pouring trick, the six of us — Gagern, F.F., Howard Fisk, Tom Hackett, Monica, and myself — got together to thrash out the question, and try to decide who had done it. Howard suggested that it might be a good idea if we accounted to each other for our movements at the time it happened."

"Alibi?"

"Yes. Tom accounted for his movements, though he hadn't any witness to them. The same applied to Howard, who had been wandering about. I told my story. Whereupon Gagern drew himself up and turned into the complete baronial stuffed-shirt. He

143

said it was intolerable. He said he really could not endure my impertinent and unwarranted interference any longer. He refused to give any account of himself; and instructed his wife to do the same. Of course F.F. obediently backed him up. As a result, I haven't been able to get a word out of her since."

"Just a minute, son," said H.M.

He seemed bothered by an invisible fly. He sniffed.

"There's one thing I'm not clear about," he went on. "Suppose all this is true? I say: supposin' it is? What's your proposition? What do you want here? This'd be a job for the police, wouldn't it? Why bombard me about it?"

Now they had come to the crux. Though he tried to be very casual, as befitted a prospective candidate for Military Intelligence, he found an annoying lump in his throat.

"Because," he replied, "Gagern is a Nazi espionage agent; and I can prove it."

"Go on, son," said H.M.

"It's a curious fact, sir, that the one thing which never rouses anybody's suspicions is a big film company shooting on location. Suppose I were a spy who wanted—in peace time, of course—to get some photographs of naval defenses. If I tried creeping about the place with a little camera, every guard in the place would be after me in two seconds. But I could roll up in grandeur with five motor-cars, two sound-recording lorries, and a battery of the biggest and finest cameras in existence: and the very admirals would pose for me.

"That is what Gagern did. In some mysterious way he managed to persuade the Admiralty to get what he

144

liked at Portsmouth, Gravesend, and Scapa Flow, as exteriors for this film *Spies at Sea*. This was before the war, naturally. Most of the stuff can never be used now in a film; the Ministry of Information would have a fit. But it was taken. Further, it was all arranged for by Gagern, though that's normally the producer's work. Lastly, there is a point which I didn't learn until this morning, from Tom Hackett. Gagern was supposed to shoot five thousand feet of film. He actually did shoot eight thousand: of which the greater part has now disappeared, leaving Albion Films wild."

(There was definitely an atmosphere in the room now. Bill Cartwright could feel it.)

"I've got just one thing more to say, sir, and then you can take what action you see fit. I tell you frankly, I'm more interested in Monica Stanton than in any question of espionage. For more than two mortal weeks, Gagern has been supposed to be confined to his house with a bad attack of 'flu. He was supposed to have caught 'flu from a dousing while directing a submarine sequence. Well, he didn't."

"Didn't what?"

"He didn't catch 'flu. He's as well as you or I."

H.M. opened one eye. "So? How do you know that?"

"Because I've stuck to his trail," returned Bill, not without relish.

"So," said H.M. thoughtfully, "you've stuck to his trail, hey?"

"Yes, sir. I have kept on that gentleman a gaze which would have embarrassed Medusa. He and F.F. have a rose-bowered cottage in the most idyllic style;

and, blackout or no blackout, I've haunted it. I don't say he has not been able to get away from me once or twice, since he was able to leave those infernal anonymous letters. But in general he hasn't been able to stir out of the house."

"He hasn't," said H.M., "been able to stir out of the house."

"No—not until Monday night. At the end of last week, unfortunately, I relaxed my vigilance. I thought the trouble was all over, though I've known his illness was a fake ever since I caught him trying to sneak out of the house on Wednesday fortnight. He opened the back door, and there I was, sitting on a garden seat and smoking my pipe."

"That's real good work, son."

"Thank you, sir. But, the moment I did relax my vigilance, there was the second attack on Monica Stanton. I'll be perfectly fair about this. I can't swear it was his voice I heard outside the windows on Monday night, shouting 'lights.' It was the queerest and most inhuman-sounding voice I ever heard; disguised somehow. "It might have been a man's or a woman's. But—"

"Uh-huh?"

"I ran outside after the swine, with a torch, just after the shot was fired. It was as black as your hat, but I heard him start to run. I lost him, unfortunately, because he was too far away. But I had one satisfaction. I chased him into the lake."

"You did what?"

"I chased him into the lake."

"You mean he fell overboard *again?*"

Bill Cartwright chuckled.

"Well, I am not in a position to swear it was Gagern, because I didn't set eyes on him. But, judging by the sound of the splash, he took such a toss as it would have done your heart good to see. I am gratified to state that it was over by the south bank of the lake, where there is a good deal of scum on the surface. He hauled himself out and got away.

"Now, sir," continued Bill, in a more serious and fitting manner, "the whole point is that I am still completely in the dark as to what his game is. I know he is an espionage agent: I think I have proved that: and I know he is responsible for the attacks on Monica. But why?

"I can't prove anything by his handwriting. That is, you can't just walk up to a person and say, 'Look here, hand over a speciman of your writing'; and subtle dodges for obtaining it are easier in fiction than in real life. I can't prove anything by his voice. The sulphuric acid was poured down the speaking-tube out of a beer bottle which I later found upstairs in the doctor's house; but it had no fingerprints because Gagern was wearing gloves. The bullet was fired out of a .38 revolver, but I haven't been able to find the gun.

"On the other hand, I cannot help taking a modest pride in my deductions, which I submit are borne out to the last detail by the facts. Believe me, I deeply appreciate the words of commendation you have been good enough to utter. If I have been able to be of any service to your department —"

He paused.

H.M. had closed both eyes.

"Listen, son," said H.M., in a gentle, powerful

whisper. "I'm not mad any longer. I'm in a soothed and soothin' state of mind. But before you go any further, lemme ask you something. Do you know why I asked you to come here?"

"No."

"You haven't got any idea?"

"Well, I thought—"

H.M. nodded to Captain Blake, who went and opened the door and called out something.

"Because there didn't seem to be any legal way of stoppin' you," said H.M. "I want you to meet a feller by the name of Kurt von Gagern, the same chap you've been talking about. His real name is Joe Collins. He's one of my men. Come on in, Joe. Sit down. Have a cigar?"

IX

H.M. got to his feet.

His corporation, ornamented with a big gold watchchain across the waistcoat, preceded him in splendor like the figurehead of a man-o'-war. He put his fists on his hips. His expression was less of wrath than of a sort of awe.

"Y'know, son," he said, "you take the cake. You do for a fact. Your ingenious notions have been causin' me more trouble than the whole German secret service. Joe says he thinks you're honest. I think you are too. I'll have the hide off your ears if you ever breathe a word of this; but I'd rather take a chance and trust you than have you chivvyin' Joe all over the landscape every time he tries to do some work . . . Here, Joe. This way."

Joe Collins, alias Kurt von Gagern, eyed Bill Cartwright with an indecipherable stare as he came in.

In his manner was that same curious tinge of exasperation which had been noticed before. In it were also embarrassment, hesitation, and perhaps dislike. He was carefully dressed, in a blue lounge suit with the tie of a good club. He had so drilled himself into his part that even here he did not forget to duck his head and click his heels together before putting his hat on the desk. His rather handsome face was composed, though the nose had become reddish.

"That's all right, Joe," said H.M. soothingly. "Just sit down and take it easy. How are you feelin' today?"

"I have a code," answered Gagern sullenly.

Though this statement was not a surprising one, it was nevertheless misleading: he meant that he had a cold.

H.M. turned to Bill.

"Now looky here," he went on. "I want you to get out of your head, once and for all, the idea that Joe had anything to do either with the acid-pourin' affair or the revolver shot through the window. He hadn't. The reason why he wouldn't account for his whereabouts at the time of the acid-pourin' was that he was talking to me on the telephone."

Bill regarded him stupidly. He had begun to feel a trifle ill.

"Talking to you? About the acid, you mean?"

"Acid? Lord love a duck, *no!* About the missin' cinema film. You're hypnotized by that acid, son. Let me ask you something. You said a minute ago that it was only today this feller Hackett told you about some of those shots at Portsmouth and Scapa Flow being missing?"

"Yes, that's right."

H.M. sniffed. "It was awful stale news, son," he said in a curious voice. "That film was pinched at the same time as the sulphuric acid. Joe here discovered it was gone. That was why he may have seemed a

150

little bit distraught, and not much concerned with acid. That was why he phoned me. Most of the missin' film won't matter so much. But there's about a hundred feet of it that'll play blue blazes if it ever gets to Germany. With it, a submarine could sneak into the base of the Grand Fleet and raise Old Harry."

H.M. was worried. He lowered his big bulk into the chair again. He picked up a pen-holder and chewed on it as though it were a cigar.

"Now," he said, "you know. I'm trustin' your word of honor to keep it to yourself who Joe is and what he's really doin'. Besides, if Joe's wife learns he's not a von-und-zu baron there'll be trouble for fair."

Bill rubbed his forehead.

"And Tom Hackett never told me—"

"No," said Gagern coldly. "After all, why should he have? It was no concern of yours."

The fact that this was true only made Bill more angry. Gagern was sitting bolt upright, his nose standing out reddish against his handsome face, and his eyes watery.

"Please understand, Mr. Cartwright," he went on, "that I was opposed to Sir Henry's telling you this. But there seemed no other way out. I did not wish to be embarrassed more than was necessary."

(You didn't?)

"My apologies all around," said Bill. He got to his feet, a sick feeling in his chest. "It seems I made a fool of myself." He looked at Gagern. "So it was you I chased into the lake on Monday night?"

"Id was," snapped Gagern.

"And so it does turn out that you were a fake after

all?"

Gagern went as white as his collar.

"If you wish to put it like that, yes."

"You're not a German baron?"

"No; nor a German. Sir Henry knew both my parents. But I was brought up by a German governess, and I am bi-lingual."

"What about your great reputation as a director with UFA? Is that a myth too?"

Gagern looked at him steadily. "I was for some months a cameraman with UFA. Times have seldom been prosperous with me, Mr. Cartwright; or happy."

There was something in the way he said this which suddenly weakened the dislike Bill had felt for him.

"Listen to me, Mr. Cartwright," he continued, with such raw sincerity that Bill squirmed. "A year ago I had nothing. I had returned from knocking round the world. I was broke and I was ill. I resolved that I would not endure this any longer. So I created for myself the character of Baron von Gagern, a German film director. I met Mr. Thomas Hackett and convinced him that I was the man he wanted. As Joseph Collins I should have been laughed at. But you shall say for yourself whether or not my work has been satisfactory."

"All right! I only—"

"In another year I should have been, perhaps shall be, the best-known director in England. That is not vanity: it is truth, and you know it. I had a comfortable place. I was married, and I love my wife. God forbid that you should ever love a woman as much as I love Frances. A year ago she would not have looked at me."

He paused, and moistened his lips.

For all the strength of his words, he was trying to speak unemotionally.

"By the middle of August it became clear to anyone who knew the Nazi mind and character that war was inevitable. I told my wife so. I could have remained where I was and who I was. No one knew me. Instead I offered my services to Sir Henry in case war should break out, and risked precisely what is happening now. If you do not keep my secret, I am done for. But I did this because twenty-three years ago I was a British agent in Germany: one of the best, I am glad to say. Ours is a humble work and perhaps you will say a dirty work. They do not give decorations for it in this country, nor do we expect any. But in France, fake or no, I am entitled to wear the Grand Cross of the Legion of Honour."

Bill bowed stiffly. It was impossible not to be infected by the formal courtesy of his manner.

"Don't worry about that," he said. "I'll keep your secret. But just tell me one thing. Why the devil did you put that water-bottle full of sulphuric acid on the *Brünhilde* set?"

"I didn't."

"But—"

Gagern nodded toward the papers on H.M.'s desk.

"I have read your reconstruction. I admired its logic even when I cursed you. The answer is that the set was originally arranged just as you see it in the photographs. It was altered by Mr. Howard Fisk, who later knocked it over. I was not within six feet of Fisk when he upset the water-bottle, as anyone who was present will tell you. I thought it best to keep quiet and see what happened."

He raised his hand in a protesting gesture. The muscles of his thin, aristocratic-looking face were working; he took out a handkerchief and rubbed the moisture from his eyes.

"One moment. I do not really suspect Fisk. That is the trouble. Great God, I do not know *whom* to suspect. It is worse than the problem of Bresemann at Zurich in 1916. There were apparently—as you say—only the six of us present. We have not one question to answer, but half a dozen. Thùs (a) who stole the cinema film?; (b) who put the acid in the water-bottle, and why?; (c) who twice attacked Miss Monica Stanton, and why?; (d) what is the reason for the personal hatred toward Miss Stanton; (e) are all these things related; and (f) if so, how?"

There was a silence.

"Well, I wish you luck," said Bill. "And now, if you'll excuse me—"

"No," grunted H.M.

There was an expression of sour and ghoulish amusement on H.M.'s face.

"Feelin' all hot and cold?" he inquired. "Burnin' sense of humiliation making you want to get out of our sight forever? No, son. That reconstruction of yours wasn't a bad piece of work, with the single error that you got the wrong man. Sit down and forget it. Maybe you can help us. Got any ideas?"

"No, sir. But may I ask a question?"

"Sure, son. Fire away."

Bill turned to Gagern. "Well, have *you* got any ideas? You see, in the blindness of my conceit I thought I had you taped. If Sir Henry vouches for you during the time Monica was attacked on the sound-stage floor, that's good enough for me. But I was congratulating myself that I could keep Monica safe because I knew the direction of the danger. And now I don't. She's downstairs now; and safe enough at the War Office; but she insists on staying at Pineham and it's driving me mad. Where do you think we ought to look? What, for instance, were you doing down by the lake on Monday night?"

Gagern placed his right hand flat on the desk, and adjusted the fingers there as though he were making fingerprints.

"If only," he said thoughtfully, "it were none of us."

"What do you mean, if it were none of us?"

"I mean," retorted Gagern, giving the desk a rap, "the fatal six. That is what I stumble over every time. I should as soon think of suspecting you or Fisk or Hackett as I should think of suspecting my own wife. Yet apparently we have to accept it. As for what I was doing near the Old Building on Monday night—"

He checked himself, and glanced inquiringly at H.M.

"It's all right, son," said H.M. "Tell him. Joe was trying to keep his eye on a gal named Tilly Parsons."

2

If H.M.'s swivel chair had moved up to the ceiling by astral levitation, and then dropped down with all its weight on Bill Cartwright's head, he could not have been more completely floored. In his books he always practiced the doctrine of the criminal being the "least likely person." To him half the savor of the game was the appalled shock with which—he hoped—the reader would be greeted at the revelation.

But this shocked him in another sense. It was incredible. It was merely fantastic.

"Tilly Parsons?" he shouted. "Why?"

"Because she is not Tilly Parsons," replied Gagern. "At least, I do not think she is the same Tilly Parsons I met once at a cocktail party in Hollywood. I have only seen her at a distance, but I am almost willing to swear to it. We have cabled Jewell Pictures at Hollywood, of course."

"And what did they say?"

"They have not replied yet."

Bill beat the air with gestures. "But Tilly wasn't even in England when—well, when the first of these things happened!"

"That is the difficulty," conceded Gagern. "She was not in England and she was certainly, so far as we can tell, not in the sound stage on the afternoon of August 23. Apparently she *cannot* have stolen the film, doctored the water bottle, or poured the acid at Miss Stanton. I do not say she is a spy or a would-be murderer. I only say she is a fraud."

The red-rimmed eyes looked steadily at Bill. Gagern's hand, a delicate hand with long fingers, tapped on the desk.

"Let me, however, ask you a question. We both heard that voice which went crying, 'Miss Stanton, lights,' outside the windows on Monday night, and lured that lady within a fraction of an inch of death. I heard it perhaps better than you, since the thickness of wall, windows, and curtains intervened between it and you."

"Well?"

"Where was Tilly Parsons then?"

"In her room."

"How do you know that? Did you see her?"

A queer, creepy sensation began to get into Bill Cartwright's chest.

"Not until after the shot was fired, no."

"How long after?"

"I'm hanged if I can remember."

"Could she (for instance) have slipped out of the window of her room, first turning out the lights so that she could not be seen from outside; could she have called out to Miss Stanton, rapped on the window, fired the shot, and slipped back in again unseen by you?"

"It would have been physically possible, yes."

"Was the door closed between her office and Miss Stanton's?"

"Yes."

"Now please think for a moment, Mr. Cartwright, and tell me whether the voice outside the window sounded familiar to you?"

Tilly's voice.

For two days he had been taunted, tormented, and put upon thorns by the note of familiarity in that voice; the harsh and husky quality underlying; the thick sound, as though of a mouth full of pebbles; the eerie bawling which might have been a man's or a woman's. It was Tilly's voice.

"One other small point. You say in your letter to Sir Henry"—Gagern moved his finger sideways—"that Miss Stanton has been troubled with anonymous letters. How do the letters reach her?"

"By hand, at the Merefield Country Club."

"So. That is interesting. And does Tilly Parsons also live at the Merefield Country Club?"

"Yes; she has the room next to . . ." Bill stopped. Anger, incredulity, bewilderment, all flooded over him with exactly the same effect as a sea-wave; and he spluttered. "I don't believe it," he said.

"Why? Because you like the lady?" asked Gagern. His face was full of cynicism; his eyes were turned inward. "I have found that that is seldom a safe rule in life. In any case, I do not say that it *is* so. For I am convinced that one person, and only one, is behind all these events; and this woman cannot have been concerned in the first part of it. She may, even, be innocently concerned in it. I only say that she will require watching. Have you any suggestion, Sir Henry?"

Throughout this H.M. had been sleepily chewing the pen-holder and making noises.

"I say," he repeated stubbornly, "that I'm interested in that missing film. And that's all I'm interested in." He sat up and howled at them. "Don't you think I got any work to do? Do you think I can sit crystal-gazin' about your murders when what I want is that film? Now let me get something straight. You say the film was stolen at the same time as the sulphuric acid?"

"No. I only tell you that we discovered their loss at the same time."

"Uh-huh. The acid was kept in the sound stage, was it? Before it got pinched, I mean?"

"Yes."

"But the film wasn't in the sound stage, I gather?"

"No, certainly not. It was in the 'Library,' which is a big storage room near the cutting and developing rooms in the east wing of the main building."

"And when, exactly, did you hear about it disappearing?"

"About a quarter to five in the afternoon. Roger Baker rang through from the Library to the sound stage and told me. I went straight to the Library: that was why nobody could find me. I found out it was true. I came back to the sound stage about five minutes past five o'clock. Tom Hackett was standing by the door, searching everybody (for acid) who went out. I went straight to a telephone and rang you up; and we were still talking when I heard a window smash at ten minutes past five—the time of the acid-pouring. I did not tell Hackett about the loss of the film until later. He was upset enough as it was."

"And who has access to this Library?"

"Anybody. We share it with Radiant Pictures and S.A.G."

H.M. eyed him curiously. "You treat things sort of careless down in that part of the world, don't you, son?"

"Unfortunately, we do."

"Well," said H.M., "I've got only one thing to say to you. You two get together and you find me that film. I don't care two hoots and a whistle for anything else. Now just you beetle off and let me get some work done. Only—" His big face smoothed itself out. An eye, small and sharp and disconcerting, swung round to Bill Cartwright. "Was it her voice, son?" he asked in a soft manner.

"Whose voice?"

"Was it Tilly Parsons' voice you heard outside the window when somebody took a pot-shot at this gal?"

"I don't know," said Bill abruptly. "I'm afraid it was."

After a silence Bill turned to Gagern.

"Monica's downstairs now," he went on. "I suggest we all have a drink and go into this. I can't believe that Tilly, of all people, is up to any funny business. But if she is—well, Monica's the person who has got to know it."

"At your service," said Gagern.

Captain Blake took them out. The last thing they saw, before the door closed, was H.M. sitting like an impassive and ill-tempered idol, piled behind his desk; and both of them had an idea that H.M. was telling less than he knew. They were let out of the War Office by a different entrance from that by which they had come in, opening into a street parallel with Horseguards Avenue on the other side; so that they had to walk all the way round the block to reach the main courtyard again. Big Ben was just striking the shock of four-thirty—a fact which later became important.

Monica was not in the anteroom.

They began to search, pushing among the crowd. They were still searching, frantically, when one of the messengers took pity on them. Bill made short work of explaining what was wrong.

"The young lady, sir?" he said to Bill. "Oh, she's

gone. She walked out of here not a minute after you went upstairs."

Up in the little office above the courtyard, growing gray with afternoon light, Sir Henry Merrivale still sat behind his desk and stared at the door. The corner of one nostril seemed to have acquired a permanent twist, as though he were smelling a bad breakfast egg.

Captain Blake closed the door, sat down on the edge of the desk, and looked at him.

"H.M.," he said, "what's the game?"

"Eh?"

"I said," repeated his companion in a louder voice, "what's the game?"

"Oh, I was just sittin' and thinkin'." H.M.'s eye wandered round the office, out into the courtyard, and over blank rows of windows. "Y'know, Ken — I'm not goin' to be here much longer."

"Nonsense!" said the other sharply.

"It's true, though. This is a young man's war, Ken. They don't sing *Tipperary* any longer. I'm nearly seventy years old: did you know that?"

"Bah."

"No, Ken; I'm not foolin' this time. I'm surprised it's lasted as long as this. In another week or so I'll be gettin' my walking-papers. And then what? I'll tell you. As sure as you live and breathe, the hyena-souled bounders are goin' to stick me straight into the House of Lords—"

Ken Blake interrupted him.

"But see here, H.M.," he argued, "I don't see any reason for such a nightmare. Masters tells me you've been going on for a long time about being treacherously sand-bagged and shoved into the House of Lords. But why? After all, it's not obligatory. Even if they do offer you a peerage, you can always politely refuse it, can't you?"

H.M. regarded him with a dreary eye.

"Oh, my son!—You're married, aren't you?"

"H'm," said the other, enlightened.

"Yes. In addition to which, I've got two marriageable daughters. Ken, what would happen to me at home if I refused a peerage just won't bear thinkin' about. It makes me wake up in a cold sweat at night when I dream about it."

He reflected.

"I'll tell you what I'm goin' to do, Ken," he declared quite seriously. "If they try any trick like that, I'll tell you exactly what I'm goin' to do. I'm going out East and enter a Trappist monastery."

"Don't be an ass!"

"I mean it, son. They got some vows I rather like. 'Chastity, poverty, and silence.' I never was very keen about chastity or poverty; but, burn me, Ken, the silence would suit me right down to the ground. Besides—"

"Besides what?"

H.M. squirmed. He glared at the pen-holder.

"Well, Ken," he mumbled uncomfortably, "I mean, we're none of us gettin' any younger. It's got to be in the nature of things. Three score years and ten. I mean to say, there comes a time in every bloke's life when he's got to think about dyin'; when he knows there can't be many more years to—"

His companion was aghast. In all the moods of grousing which had ever beset H.M., and the name of them was legion, he had never before gone as far as this.

"Drop it," Captain Blake said sharply.

H.M. continued to shake his head.

"Well, Ken, y'know—"

"I said drop it. I know exactly what's wrong with you. In the first place, they're not going to retire you. Even if they do, you've still got more intelligence in that nut of yours than the whole crowd of them put together."

"That's what you think."

"In the second place, you had lunch with the Home Secretary and that's practically fatal. In the third place"—here he looked hard at H.M.—"the final point is that you'd give your ears to go down to Pineham and find out what's really going on in that film studio."

H.M. glowered at him.

"That," insisted Captain Blake, "is why I asked you a minute ago: What's the game?"

"Game? There's no game."

"H.M., that won't do. I know you. You're determined to be the Old Maestro if it chokes you. What exactly is up? This fellow Gagern, or Collins, for instance . . ."

"Joe? What about him?"

"Well, is this the double-twist? Do you think Gagern is the film-stealing serpent, and are you giving him a clean bill of health in order to catch him?"

H.M. shook his head. "No, son," he said seriously. "Joe is absolutely trustworthy: he's no more a spy than I am. I was not thinkin' about that. Only—"

"Only what?"

H.M. pointed to the mass of loose papers on his desk. He ran his hands among them and threw them about him, scrabbling among them like an elderly cockerel in a barnyard.

"It's rummy," he roared. "All this is, It smells of rumminess to high heaven. If there were ever a rummier case than this to come and pitch on my desk, this case is that case. Have you read any of this testimony?"

"No."

"Have a look at it, then. At this. And this." Papers flew. "Y'know, Ken, I doubt if any of 'em down there has the ghost of an idea what's really going on. And, if my notion happens to be right, it's nasty. It's uncommon nasty. I only hope this fellow Cartwright has got that gal safe and sound. Because the person behind this business has now stopped foolin'. It'll be murder next, Ken: murder with the gloves off, and no mistake made when the punch goes home."

"What are you going to do?"

For a time H.M. did not speak. He sat back and twiddled his thumbs, his lowering gaze fixed on the door. The long afternoon light drew in across the courtyard of the War Office. Presently H.M. shook his head. He reached out and picked up the telephone.

"Get me Scotland Yard," he said.

X

It was nearly three o'clock when Monica Stanton walked out of the War Office.

Again truth must be told. At this moment she had no intention of going back to Pineham. She was in no mood for work. What she meant to do was: first, go to Bond Street and buy a lot of new clothes as balm for her angry soul; and, second, go to the Café Royal and get herself picked up by the first attractive man she met.

Why she thought of the Café Royal it would be difficult to say. Lady Astor herself would have difficulty in finding any wickedness at that innocent and indeed exemplary place. But Monica remembered that her Aunt Flossie had once spoken darkly of it. And at least you met a decent class of people there — whereas you never knew what trouble you might find if you went (for instance) to Soho.

"Ee!" said Monica to herself, in fury.

In other words, she had reached that state of mind in which no girl, of however lofty character, is safe to be allowed loose.

And Monica's character, basically, was anything but lofty.

She hailed a taxi in Whitehall. Bill Cartwright had done that deliberately, of course, to humiliate her. He had known all along she would never be allowed into the War Office.

Her mind dwelt with hatred on the picture of Bill as he probably was now. He would be sitting in a spacious office, all mahogany and deep carpets, with bronze busts on bookcases, and an Adam fireplace. He would be drinking whisky-and-soda—Monica herself, when she reached the Café Royal, was going to have absinthe—and listening to some thrilling anecdote of the Secret Service, told by a tall gray man with a deep voice, who sat at a desk with his back to the Adam fireplace.

Every film-goer knows that this is a true picture of the Military Intelligence Department; and Monica elaborated it until pukka sahibs abounded.

For a second or two she considered the idea of rapping on the glass and asking the taxi-driver to take her to some place that was really low. She had heard that taxi-drivers knew about such things. And that she did not do this was due not to the training of Canon Stanton, but to a disquieting feeling that three o'clock in the afternoon was all wrong: it was unromantic: what she wanted was soft lights, and plush, and an Edwardian atmosphere.

And Bill Cartwright?

At Pineham, for instance—

This was the point at which Monica, her thoughts returning to Pineham for the first time in hours, sat up in the cab with a feeling of something like horror.

It was Wednesday afternoon.

For days, and even weeks, she had had an engagement for this Wednesday afternoon. For days, even weeks, it had been arranged that on Wednesday afternoon she should meet Mr. Hackett and Mr. Fisk in her office, to show them the script as far as she had written it. She had spoken about it to Howard Fisk on Monday night. The recollection struck her to sheer panic. Yet under the treacherous blandishments of Bill Cartwright, under the hypnosis of the Military Intelligence Department and the glory that went therewith, she had until this moment clean forgotten about it.

Monica flung open the glass panel of the taxi.

"Marylebone Street station, quick!" she said to the driver.

2

There was no train, of course, until a quarter past four.

Monica paced the platform. She passed the bookstall so many times that she wondered whether the proprietor was beginning to suspect her of shoplifting designs on the Penguins. While the hands of the clock crawled from three-fifteen to three-thirty, she pictured Messrs. Hackett and Fisk sitting at Pineham with their watches in front of them: getting madder and madder, and finally deciding to give her the sack.

She gulped a cup of tea in the buffet. She weighed

herself. Finally, she remembered that red leather Victorian needlework box, in which she kept cigarettes on the desk in her office, was now empty; and—a fact which was shortly to prove of the utmost importance—she bought cigarettes.

Monica Stanton bought a box of fifty Players at the station tobacconist's, and put it into her handbag without opening it.

Three-forty. Ten minutes to four. The hour itself. She was through the platform barrier the instant it was opened, and waited ten more mortal minutes before the departure of the train. At five o'clock she was put down, aching, in the stillness and cool at Pineham station.

"Punctuality," Mr. Thomas Hackett had once said, "has been called the politeness of kings. It's more than that: it's plain good business. Now, I'm always punctual myself, and I can't tolerate unpunctuality in other people. When I find it—"

The usual station taxi, which took you to Pineham Studios for the modest sum of one and sixpence, was missing. Monica set out on foot along the well-worn path over the open fields.

By the time she reached the grounds, she was running. The shortest way down to the Old Building, she calculated, was to take the path behind the main building and go down over the lawns. She was hurrying along this path, which had the sound-stages on the left of it and a rail-fence on the right, when abruptly, she solved one of the small mysteries which had been perplexing her since the start.

On the rail-fence sat a venerable-looking old gentleman, with gray side-whiskers and a cocked hat;

he wore the scarlet and gold court-dress of the early nineteenth century, and was smoking a pipe. Beside him sat the Archbishop of Canterbury, reading the *Daily Express*. Three or four officers of the Scots Greys kept a respectable distance from them, and from two other men who stood in the middle of the path.

One was a short fat man with a cigar, the other a tall bespectacled young man with an ultra-refined accent.

"Lookit," said the fat man. "They can't do this to me. What do you mean, we can't shoot the Battle of Waterloo? We *got* to shoot the Battle of Waterloo. All we got to do is shoot the Battle of Waterloo, and the picture is finished."

"I am sorry, Mr. Aaronson, but I am afraid it will be impossible. The British army has been called up."

"I still don't get it. What do you mean, called up?"

"The British army were real soldiers, Mr. Aaronson, lent to us by the authorities. They have been called up for active service."

"What about the French army?"

"The French army, Mr. Aaronson, has enlisted for Home Defense. Napoleon is now serving as an Air Raid Warden."

"Well, Jeez, we got to do something! Get extras to do it."

"It would be difficult to train them at such short notice, Mr. Aaronson."

"I don't want 'em trained. I want 'em to fight the Battle of Waterloo. Lookit, though. Wait a minute. I got an idea. Do you think maybe we could finish the picture and just not have the Battle of Waterloo in it at all?"

"I fear it will be imperative, Mr. Aaronson."

"Then here's how we do it," said the fat man. "We do it symbolically, see? The Duke of Wellington is lying wounded on his camp-bed, see? He hears cannon. Biff! Bam! Zowie!"

"Yes, Mr. Aaronson?"

"The tears are streaming down his face, see? He says, 'There are the brave boys mixing it out there, and I can't help 'em.' Maybe in his delirium he sees a vision of the future, see? Jeez, look! This'll be artistic as hell. The Duke of Wellington—"

Monica Stanton stopped dead.

She only partly heard the fat man's inspired words, just as she only saw him in connection with another person. Along the path was coming the page-boy, Jimmy, who guarded the door to sound stage number three. He was released from duty, and eating a chocolate bar. Monica knew now where she had seen him before.

She maneuvered him into a corner.

"Jimmy," she said.

"Yes, miss?"

"Jimmy, do you know what my name is?"

"Sure, miss. You're Miss Stanton."

"Yes, Jimmy," said Monica. "But how did you know who I was three weeks ago, when I first came here? You were supposed to give a message to 'the lady who came in with Mr. Cartwright': that was what it said on the blackboard. How did you know I was the lady who came in with Mr. Cartwright?"

" 'Cos I sawyer come into the sound stage with Mr. Cartwright, miss."

"No, you didn't, Jimmy."

"Miss?"

"You weren't in the sound stage then," said Monica. "I know where I saw you. When Mr. Cartwright and I got to the main building, you were just coming out of the canteen, eating a chocolate bar."

"I dunno whatcher mean, miss. S'helpme, I don't."

"Yes, you do. I remember now. You didn't see us, because your back was toward us, and we went straight through. You couldn't have seen us. So how did you know I was the lady who came in with Mr. Cartwright, and how did you know what my name was?"

"S'helpme, miss—"

Jimmy addressed the sky so passionately that the present chocolate bar flew out of his hand. He regarded it with consternation; then he pounced on it and dusted it off. This, he felt, was the heaping measure of injustice. To bring up something that happened three weeks ago, which was as a thousand years into the dim past and which he himself had forgotten, was the sort of unfair trick they were always playing on you.

"Jimmy, I'm not going to tell on you," urged Monica. "I know you aren't supposed to leave the sound stage, but I'm not going to tell anybody."

"I told Mr. Cartwright the day afterward—"

"Never mind what you told Mr. Cartwright. Come on, Jimmy. Tell me. I'm not going to tell anybody."

"Criss-cross and hope to die?"

"Criss-cross."

"Well," said Jimmy, licking clean one corner of the chocolate bar, and sullenly starting afresh, "I asked

Miss Fleur. Crumbs, miss, I didn't mean anything! I wasn't gone more'n a minute or two. I came back, and there was the message, and how was I to know who you were? So I ast Miss Fleur. I met her over by Eighteen-eighty-two, and I ast her. She told me. She was drinking beer."

"She was drinking *what?*"

"Well, she had a beer bottle in her hand," Jimmy defended himself, "and she looked funny. I ast Corky O'Brien did he think she was a secret drinker. He said he expected she took dope, more like. His old man's a hop-head, so he ought to know."

"Jimmy!"

"O.K., miss; skip it."

The Rev. Canon Stanton had once preached a powerful sermon on the insidious influence of American talking pictures on the youth of Great Britain. Monica evidently did not share these views: she crossed Jimmy's palm with silver.

Anyway, she had undoubtedly missed Messrs. Hackett and Fisk now. She stood at the top of the hill, looking down toward the Old Building in the shallow green valley, and her feelings were bitter. She could not understand why it had seemed so very important to find out where she had seen that pageboy before. It had seemed so; for three weeks it had nagged at her subconscious mind; but why? After all, she did not suspect Jimmy of—

Of having poured fiery acid into her face, or fired a bullet at that face from a few feet away.

It was twenty minutes past five o'clock. Though the sky to the west was still clear and mellow, the Old Building had begun to retreat into shadow. Birds bickered in the vines outside it. This was the first time, it occurred to Monica, she had been at Pineham without having Bill Cartwright within call in case she needed help.

But there was Tilly: Tilly was a host in herself.

Descending the hill, Monica went into the Old Building. The writers' rooms were in a corridor branching off immediately to your right as you entered the front door. You went up three indoor steps; and the corridor, brown linoleum and white walls, stretched away to an elm-shaded window at the far end. First there was Tilly's room, then Monica's, and then Bill's.

Monica met nobody: the porter on duty in the lobby had gone. In passing she tapped at Tilly's door, but she got no reply.

Her own office was also empty. It lay neat and swept and dusky in the afternoon light, with the gleam of the lake beyond the windows. The rubber cover was on the typewriter; manuscript lay in a trim sheaf held down by a book.

Monica glanced instinctively in the direction of the bullet-hole in the wall, which she had covered with a calendar. Then her eyes, deceived for the first time, flew back toward the typewriter.

There was something lying on top of the rubber. It was a squarish envelope, pink in color, addressed with blue-black ink in a handwriting which was only too familiar. Evil, breathing malice as clearly as though someone had whispered aloud in the room, was another anonymous letter.

If Monica had been asked how she really felt about the persecution of the past weeks, she would have answered that she refused to think about it. And this in a sense was true. She did not think about it: she only fought it. Just as Miss Flossie Stanton could not have prevented her from writing the book she wanted to write, so her anonymous friend at Pineham could not drive her away from here.

But in her heart she was frightened of Miss Flossie. And she was a hundred times more frightened of the person who used sulphuric acid.

She went over to her desk, tore open the envelope, and read the letter.

Who was sending these things? What difference did that make? Somebody was; and the very feel of the letters to the touch was unpleasant. This particular one was no better or no worse that the first two, except for the last two lines.

It's all up now. You will be seeing me soon in the flesh, Bright-eyes. And will you be surprised?

For a time Monica did not move. Her cheeks felt hot and her heart had begun to beat with slow, heavy rhythm.

"Tilly!" she called out.

There was no reply.

"Tilly!" stormed Monica.

Still clutching her handbag under her arm, she

went to the communicating door, tapped on it, and opened it. The other office was empty, but Tilly could not be far away.

A hissing, bumping noise of steam in a kettle issued from the partly open door of the cloak-room in the far right-hand corner of Tilly's office. Tilly, as usual, was boiling water for one of her eternal pots of coffee. As usual, she had forgotten it: which she did on an average of half a dozen times a day, until a denser and more acrid cloud of steam warned her that she was burning the bottom out of the kettle.

Monica went to the cloak-room, and turned off the gas-ring. The bottom of the kettle was not burnt through, though its metal, white-hot, had a powdery flakiness. Not a pleasant sight.

"Tilly!" Monica cried amid the steam.

She burnt her fingers on the kettle, and pushed it aside. In the wall over the gas-ring was a panel, once a service-hatch in the days when the Old Building had been a country house. Monica thought she heard a step outside it. She drew back the panel and glanced out, but there was nothing except the darkening corridor.

Monica left the cloak-room. This must stop. She must go up straightaway to Mr. Hackett's office on the floor above (if he were still there), and apologize. This must *stop*. She walked back past Tilly's desk in the middle of the room, and in doing so she bumped against the standing ashtray which got in your way beside the desk. The ashtray tilted and spun; its glass dish clattered; Monica caught it as it fell; and, in that flash of revelation, her heart jumped into her throat.

She was looking down at the half-open drawer of

175

Tilly's desk. Setting right the ashtray, Monica first took a quick glance round, and then dragged open the drawer. There were some untidy typed sheets of manuscript inside, scored and interlined with corrections in blue pencil. One line of writing curved up and ran clear along the side of the paper.

Monica stared at that sheet of manuscript.

Then she picked up the sheet, and ran with it into the other room. Dumping her handbag on the desk, she put the sheet of manuscript on the typewriter. She held the anonymous letter beside it.

They were the same.

Tilly's handwriting.

Very quietly, rather dazedly, Monica drew out the chair and sat down. She felt that she had to do something, to act somehow, against the nightmare that was closing in. She acted in a mechanical way to keep herself from thinking. Opening her handbag to get a handkerchief, her fingers slid over the cellophane wrapper of the box of cigarettes she had bought at the station.

Her eye next fell on the red leather needlework box, in which she kept cigarettes, beside the typewriter. She opened it. It was empty, and she turned it upside down to shake out a few loose crumbs of tobacco. She tore off the cellophane wrapping of the fifty Players, emptied them into the needlework box, and, with prickling fingers, began to arrange them in neat rows.

Tilly Parsons.

She felt a slight shudder: the thing which is known as the sensation of someone walking over your grave. It might have been a real grave. Maybe it still would be. It had never once occurred to her to suspect Tilly. And, she thought with hot-and-cold satisfaction, it had never occurred to Bill Cartwright either. Even if he tried to get specimens of handwriting from everybody at Pineham, he would never even think of looking at Tilly's.

It was growing darker in the room. She must get out of here. She must go somewhere.

"Hello, dearie," cried Tilly in the flesh, suddenly flinging the door open with a crash, and bursting into the room. "Did you have a good time in London?"

4

Tilly, bright and alert as usual, gave evidence of having had her bobbed hair permanently waved that afternoon. Her wrinkled face beamed guilelessly at Monica.

"Just hopped upstairs for a minute," she said. "I thought I put the kettle on before I left, but blessed if I can remember whether I did or not. I've been—" She stopped. "Here, honey, what's the matter with you? You're as white as a ghost."

"Go away," said Monica. "Don't come near me."

She got up, knocking over her chair with a noise which sounded louder in her ears than it really was. Tilly's voice went up a note.

"What's happened, honey? What's wrong?"

"You know what's wrong."

"I swear I don't, honey! Here, let me—"

"Go *away!*"

Monica, moving slowly, had backed across the room until her hands behind her touched the sill of the window. The hoarseness of Tilly's voice had reached a pitch which in her ears sounded horrible. Tilly waddled forward. Her eye fell on the two sheets of paper across the typewriter, and she stopped. She looked at Monica and then back at the two sheets.

The silence went on unendurably.

"So you've found out," said Tilly, keeping her head down. "I was afraid you would."

"You . . . wrote . . . those . . . letters."

"As God is my judge," said Tilly, suddenly lifting her head and looking Monica in the eyes. "As God is my judge, I never did."

"Don't you come near me," said Monica, pretty steadily. "I'm not afraid of you. Only — *why* did you do it? I've never done anything to you. I liked you. Why did you do it?"

Even now she was stunned by the fierce sincerity of Tilly's manner. Tilly's manner, in fact, had reached that pitch of high-flown and impossible melodrama which is often the surest sign of good faith. Uprearing her ample bosom, Tilly lifted her right hand as though she were taking an oath; the flabby flesh sagged in folds at her wrist.

"As I hope to live and die, as I hope to answer to the Good Man in heaven, I never wrote those letters! I know it looks like my writing. *Do* I know it? What do you think I've been thinking ever since you started to get them? I've been going nuts. I can't eat. I can't sleep. I can't — "

She put her hand to her throat.

"Wondering if you recognized the writing. Wondering if you thought it was me. Not daring to ask you. I *had* to give one of 'em to Bill Cartwright; I just *had* to. I had to know what was going on, don't you see that? If he'd asked me, I'd have told him; but I didn't dare tell him straight out in case you'd think it *was* me. I didn't do it, honey. I swear to God I didn't do it. Look, honey—"

Tilly, breathing like a horse, took a few steps forward. Monica moved away until she was touching the wall of the cloak-room, and Tilly stopped. All emotion, either passion or wheedling, seemed to collapse in her, leaving her spent and wrinkled like a toy balloon. Her voice became a dreary croak. Picking up the overturned chair, she set it right and flopped down on it. She wiped her eyes, blinked, and grew calm.

"Well, that's that," she said. "If you won't believe me, you won't. Where do we go from here?"

And she peered about the room, absently, during another silence.

Against all reason, Monica felt a twinge of doubt.

"But they're your writing! Look at it. Do you deny that they're your writing?"

"I do, honey," returned Tilly. "Because they're not."

"They even sound like you. I—I've been trying to think all along who the phrasing of them reminded me of; and it's you."

"I expect they do, honey," said Tilly indifferently, continuing to blink and peer round the room as though the matter were of no interest to her. "I expect they were meant to."

179

"Meant to?"

"That's what I said, honey."

"But do you know anybody who could imitate your handwriting? Or would want to?"

"Yes," replied Tilly, with a certain grimness. "I know one person. But that person . . . Sh-h!"

Footsteps, light and precise as of a woman who walks well, could be heard coming down a distant staircase. The footsteps passed the mouth of the corridor, hesitated, and turned in. Someone, as though to exercise a fine and deep contralto voice, was humming an experimental bar or two of a song.

"Ditch those papers!" hissed Tilly, making a striking movement like a snake. Tilly was again all action. She swept up the manuscript sheet and the letter, stuffed them into the drawer of Monica's desk, and slammed the drawer shut as there was a light rap at the corridor door.

"Hello," smiled Frances Fleur, putting her head in. In the gloom she seemed surprised and a trifle annoyed when she saw Tilly. "Do you mind if I come in, Monica? I have a very important message for you."

XI

"It's very dark in here," continued Miss Fleur. "Do you mind?"

A light-switch clicked beside the door.

Frances Fleur was one of those people who always bring excitement with them because it was a sort of excitement merely to sit and look at her. She incited what young ladies in the ninepennies had been overheard to describe as a "goosey feeling." And this was not personality: it was sheer good looks, animated by the expression of the eyes.

The face haunted you. On the screen you could not look away from it. In private life, with color to make it more alive, it was at times startling. Such was the effect when she turned on the light in Monica's office, and blinked and smiled against it. Tilly Parsons suddenly resembled a rag doll after a rain. Even Monica would have had nobody's eye except Bill Cartwright's.

Monica was partly used to her by now. She catalogued the woman's clothes: powder-blue; two-piece; silver fox at the sleeves. Summer-felt hat, of the same blue color, shading the side of the face. Black suède shoes, black handbag, and gloves. Yet even Monica felt the disturbing wave of her presence.

"This is the first time I've been in here." Frances Fleur smiled. "It's a comfortable place to work in, isn't it? May I sit down?

"Please do. Try the couch."

Miss Fleur moved across. She made the room look dingy; she stirred the air, and made it impossible to look anywhere else but at her.

"I've got two messages for you," she told Monica. "The first is from Tom and Howard. They're terribly sorry, but they simply couldn't come to see you this afternoon. They say you must be cursing them, but they couldn't help it." She looked at the ceiling. "They've been up in Tom's office all afternoon, arguing, and I've just got away from them. What's the matter, dear? Why are you laughing? What's so funny?"

"You mean *they* didn't—?"

"No, dear. They couldn't. I say, don't laugh like that; you make me nervous. They've finally come to a decision about *Spies at Sea*." The expressive eyes, never quite telling everything, moved round toward Tilly for the first time. "And that's rather a bit of good news for you."

"Is it?" said Tilly. "Why?"

Tilly had been regarding her with a stiffness which indicated ill-concealed dislike.

"Because you can go back to America now," said Miss Fleur. "I think they've decided they will stick to the original script after all. You don't mind terribly, do you?"

182

Tilly stared at her. There passed across her face an expression of real malignancy: a new expression: one which it was just as well that Monica did not notice.

"Mind?" Tilly said, from deep in her throat. "Me? Hell, no! Suit yourself. I've had my money: *I* should worry." Her color went up. "If you want the goods, I can deliver 'em. If you don't want the goods, then good-bye and good luck and good-day to ye."

"I knew you'd understand." The long-lashed eyes, at which Monica could not stop looking, returned; but not before they had given Tilly a long, speculative glance. "And that's good news," Miss Fleur went on, "because now we shall be finished with it in a few days. And then—if Tom Hackett keeps to his production schedule—I can play Eve D'Aubray in *Desire*. Won't that be nice?"

"Mind!" growled Tilly under her breath.

"I'm terribly keen about the part. Did you know, Miss Parsons, that Monica wrote it expressly for me?"

"The name is Tilly," said Tilly. "For Pete's sake, don't call me Miss Parsons. I hate it."

"Well, if you insist: Tilly. But did you know Monica wrote the part for me? A real *femme fatale,* and apparently I'm It."

"You mean you have It," snarled Tilly. "But why parade it all over the place all the time? Why—" She checked herself, swallowing, and drew the back of her hand shakily across her forehead. "Sorry. Forget it. I've got the jitters. What's a *femme fatale?*"

Miss Fleur's voice was wry.

"Something I'm afraid I shall never be," she smiled, with a look which made Monica writhe. It is all very well to write an imaginary biography of a person; but, when the original of that biography sits down to read it in cold print, the result is apt to prove embarrassing for the author.

"Tell me, my dear," Miss Fleur went on, in a slightly different voice. "I've read it clear through, you know, since I met you. I know you'll forgive my asking, but I really am curious. *Was* it all just imagination? You look terribly young, you know, and—other things. Tell me. Just between ourselves. Did you ever really . . ."

"Oh, Lord, yes," said Monica. "Thousands of times," she added wildly.

"You did?"

"Oh, Lord, yes."

"But where?"

"At home, of course," said Monica.

That the shattered photograph of Canon Stanton did not, at this moment, leap up out of the drawer of Monica's desk, may be ascribed rather to the inexorability of the law of gravity than to the damage done to abstract truth.

But Monica was not herself. Much as she liked Miss Fleur, she wished her guest would go. Her mind was on anonymous letters to the exclusion of everything else. Yet, curiously enough, Frances Fleur seemed to be feeling much the same restlessness as herself. Miss Fleur's well-shod foot had begun to tap the floor. She kept glancing at her wrist-watch.

"Have you, indeed?" she said "What a place it must be. It's near Watford."

"Yes, that's right. East Roystead, Hertfordshire. It's near Watford."

"Is that so? Do you know, I have some cousins . . ." Miss Fleur laughed, and her tone hardly changed. "Aren't you going out for dinner tonight, Miss Par — Tilly, I mean?"

"Dinner?" said Tilly. "Certainly. But not yet. It's not six o'clock yet."

"A quarter past six, I make it," corrected Monica.

"Dear, dear. Is it as late as that? I must be running along myself." Frances Fleur stirred, but did not get up. "I only dropped in to pass the time of day. After all, I mustn't interrupt your work. Er — you have some work to do, haven't you, Miss — Tilly?"

"Not any longer," said Tilly. "You tell me they've just given me the air. *I* should work? Haw, haw, haw."

This time their guest did get up. She smiled, but with her mouth alone. Her voice had that deliberate, honeyed sweetness she used at the beginning of her love-scenes.

"I told you I had two messages to give Monica," she remarked. "Would you mind terribly if we were left alone while I gave her the second one?"

It was touch and go.

Tilly stared at her.

"I can take a hint," Tilly said slowly. "It's got to be broad, you understand. It can't be subtle, or it'll go straight over my head. But I can take a hint."

"Thank you so much."

"Would I mind . . ." began Tilly.

The full power of her state of mind was not apparent until she had left them. Tilly went to her room with quiet, bouncing, dignified little steps. Once inside, after giving them a long and slow look, she slammed the door with a crash which must have been audible at the main building up the hill; and which, if this house had not been so solidly built, would have brought plaster down from the ceiling.

"Listen, quick," urged Frances Fleur, whose manner had instantly changed again. It was difficult to believe that there could be so much animation in her. "That second message was from Bill Cartwright. He's on his way out here in a taxi."

"In a taxi?"

"Yes. He was in town. He rang me up on the phone in Tom's outer office. He said I was the only person here he could trust. He made me promise not to tell Tom or Howard; but of course they got it out of me."

Miss Fleur made a face.

"Here's what Bill says you're to do. He says you're to — That woman's listening at the door," she added abruptly.

The knob of the door quivered; Monica could have sworn Tilly was just on the point of flinging it open to stalk out and deny that she was listening.

Miss Fleur got up from the couch. Soundless on the linoleum-covered brick floor, she moved over to the desk. She stood with her back to Monica, one hand on the desk and the other hand on the needle-work box: red-painted fingernails against red leather. She watched the door, and Monica watched it too. But there appeared to be no further sign of activity inside.

Then she turned round, the light shining down on blue cloth and silver fox fur. She came back softly, took Monica's hand, and made her sit down on the couch.

"Listen, Monica," she said. (Monica had not yet got over the faint thrill of being called by her first name.) "Bill said that if you got back here when it was getting dark, you were on no account to try to get home. Sh-h!"

"Yes?"

"He said that you were *on no account* to leave this building or this room until he got here. He said he was phoning to that groundkeeper, O'Brien or whatever his name is, to come in here and sit with you until he (I mean Bill) got here."

"But—"

"Sh-h! Above everything else," Miss Fleur leaned closer to whisper, "Whatever else you did, you were not to be a minute alone with," her head inclined significantly toward the door, "that woman. Do you understand?"

"I don't know.

Miss Fleur released her hand and got up. The tone of her whisper was faintly querulous.

"I'm sure I don't know what's going on. And I don't think I want to. If half what I hear is true, you must have led a very queer life indeed. All I know is that I'm frightened too. Now promise me: will you do what Bill Cartwright tells you to do?"

Not a very long time ago, Monica would instantly have said no. The negative came into her mind; she opened her mouth to speak it, and stopped. It occurred to her, with painful clarity, that the finest sight she could think of in this world would be the sight of Bill Cartwright storming into that room.

She moistened her lips.

"All right," she said. "I'll do it."

"You promise?"

"I promise."

2

Miss Fleur relaxed. A sort of radiance grew again about her, kindling the dark amber eyes which (it occurred to Monica as an unromantic comparison) were exactly the color of one of Bill's pipestems. She laughed. She smoothed her gloves. Her voice grew natural again.

"Well, I only dropped in to pay my respects," she explained, in a tone intended for the other room. "I'd love to stay, only I'm driving in to town to meet Kurt. Tom! Don't jump about so! I say, must you sneak up on everybody?"

It would not be true to say that Thomas Hackett sneaked up, since his voice was audible in the hall. But he looked very grave as he nodded to Monica, and beckoned to Howard Fisk in the hall behind him.

"I—er—thought I'd come and see you," said Mr. Hackett. He consulted his watch, and consulted it again. "Frances explained to you, did she—er—?"

"About your not being here today? Of course, Mr. Hackett. I quite understand."

"No, no," said the producer. His manner was hasty. "I mean: yes, yes. That is to say, something else has come up. Old O'Brien is down here from the main building, and he's brought some news. Miss Stanton, I'd like to ask you a question. You haven't

188

gone to the police about anything that's happened here, have you?"

Monica opened her eyes.

"The police? No, certainly not. Why?"

"Because there's a police officer here now," the other said grimly. "He's up at the main building with Mr. Marshlake."

"Tom, you always do get so upset about trifles," Miss Fleur told him, with an air of kindly weariness. "Suppose there is? There always is, it seems to me. It's probably about leaving cars out in the road again."

"Not this time," grunted Mr. Hackett. "His name is Masters, and he's a chief inspector from Scotland Yard."

It was extraordinary what an instant and deep effect the mention of that name had. If they had all been boys caught in an apple-orchard, with a bull on one side of the fence and an angry farmer on the other, they could not have looked at each other differently. Even Howard Fisk seemed disturbed. Shaking his head, he went over and sat down on Monica's desk.

Mr. Hackett addressed her impressively.

"Look here, Miss Stanton. I know how you feel. I know what you've been through. Nobody wants to see this hound caught more than I do. In fact, we've decided that you're too much of a time-bomb, and that for your own safety it would be better if we — er — severed relations. But believe me, to drag the police into a thing like this is fatal. I've had ten years' experience, and I know. I know Mr. Marshlake will think so too."

("It would be better if we — er — severed relations." Bill! Bill! Where was Bill?)

"But I didn't go to the police!" insisted Monica. "I don't know what you're talking about. Who is Mr. Marshlake anyway?"

Mr. Hackett drew a deep breath.

"He's my boss," he answered, simply but eloquently. "He wants to see Howard and me up there straight-away."

There was a silence.

The producer fiddled with his cuffs and straightened his necktie. He was evidently making a determined effort to stoke up his spirits. And so he smiled at Monica.

"Never mind," he said. "Cheer up. We're all your friends, Miss Stanton, and we'll see that the right thing is done. But what with stealing some of the finest exterior shots ever made, and everything that's happened in the past, and now this, I'm beginning to think somebody has a personal grudge against me as well as you. We'll have to go, Howard. Er — Frances" He jerked his head toward the other office. "Did you mention to Tilly Parsons . . . ?"

Miss Fleur made up her face.

"About being free to go home? Yes, Tommy darling. I've done the dirty work for you."

"Nonsense! I must have a word with her now. She can go as soon as she finishes Sequence E. We've wasted enough time with this film as it is."

"Now you're talking, my lad," interposed Howard Fisk, coming to life out of a brown study, and putting down a paper-knife with which he had been playing. "When you really get down to it and stop

190

fooling, there's nobody in the business who can hold a candle to you. Well, shall we go and face the Minotaur?"

"Yes. You'd better come too, Miss Stanton."

"I'm sorry," said Monica calmly. "I am staying here."

They looked at her.

"Bill Cartwright," said Monica. At mention of the name, her throat felt tight and her chest hurt her. "Bill asked me to stay here, and I am going to stay."

The other three exchanged a glance. Mr. Hackett's eyebrows went up in a worried way.

"Bill! I didn't think he was—er—very popular with you. Besides, what's Bill got to do with this? You come along with us. You'll be safer."

"Isn't a man named O'Brien supposed to be here with me?"

Mr. Hackett rubbed his forehead. "Maybe you're right," he admitted. "If this detective doesn't actually see you, maybe I can smooth him over and he'll get to blazes out of here. Yes, maybe you're right about that. Only: be careful. It's getting so I've got you on my conscience. O'Brien! Hoy! You can come in now." He looked round him uneasily, as Frances Fleur who was smiling and at Howard Fisk who was grim. He hesitated. "You'd better draw those blackout curtains," he said.

3

The clock was now ticking toward murder.

A careful design, arranged small bit by small bit

throughout the weeks, each bit sliding noiselessly into its proper place unobserved as the days passed, was now complete. It remained only to touch the switch, and that would be in a few minutes.

Monica, of course, knew nothing of this. She had never felt safer than when she waited in her office, with the burly O'Brien (a mustached ex-service-man who reminded her of the messenger at the War Office) sitting on the couch and reading an evening paper.

It was twenty-five minutes past seven. Monica still waited. Long ago the mutter of voices in Tillly's room, where Tilly talked to Hackett and Fisk, had faded. They had gone stamping and laughing out. As soon as they were gone, Tilly flung open the door.

"Honey—"

Ex-Corporal O'Brien cleared his throat noisily, shifted, and crackled the newspaper.

"I see, miss," he said, without looking up, "where it says here in the paper that the old Boche has . . ."

Tilly looked at him. Then she looked at Monica.

"Honey," she said, "will you come in here just a minute, please?"

"If you've got anything to say, Tilly can't you say it in here?"

"No, I can't."

"Why not?"

"Because I can't. Oh, honey, don't be such a sap! Stop this foolishness and come in here!"

"Not when you talk like that, Tilly."

Tilly's eyes opened wide.

"Are you coming in here, or aren't you?"

"No, I'm not."

The door slammed.

Its noise made Monica wince. This might be foolish and nonsensical; but she was beginning to be worried not about herself, but about Bill Cartwright. Even though night-driving conditions were bad in the blackout, he should have been here by this time.

Suppose he had had an accident? Suppose two cars had collided, and he had been thrown through the glass? And why must he take a taxi when a train would have done as well? He shouldn't fling his money about like that. And yet she could not help liking him more for doing it; it brought a glow of pleasure that, whatever else he might be, he wasn't mean. . . .

She had treated him badly; she admitted that. There came into her mind pictures of all the times when he had behaved with studious patience, smiling at her, and she had behaved like a little devil. She hadn't meant to behave like that. She wasn't really like that at all, if she could only show him.

The minutes ticked on. Tilly muttered behind the closed door, and the rattle of Tilly's typewriter began. The bright light hurt Monica's eyes. She wrapped a paper shade round the bulb. The red leather cigarette-box shone beneath it; she reached out her hand to take a cigarette, and decided against it.

Well, she was in love with him: that was all. It was a funny feeling: like exhilaration and obedience put together. Not at all what she had ascribed to Eve D'Aubray in the book, and yet a good deal like it too. If he would only *get* here, she would tell him so. Or, if she didn't exactly tell him, she would let him know beyond any doubt —

Her ear caught, from some distance away, the sound of the footsteps on the gravel path leading up to the Old Building.

The footsteps approached, and crunched louder. They must be his. They went up the steps. She heard them in the lobby. They came down the corridor.

It was Bill, right enough.

And he was mad.

She realized, as she saw him standing in the doorway, that she had never seen him genuinely mad before. The other times had not been real anger. They had been literary grouses or grouses at the universe, in which he struck a pose and boiled with high-flown phrases as much from enjoyment of using words as from anything else.

But now he was furious; and she knew it. She felt a little apprehensive and at the same time curiously pleased. She wanted him to be angry because she had deserted him at the War Office. She wanted to tell him she was sorry. She would glory in telling him she was sorry.

Bill got a grip on himself. His first words, spoken in a tone of cold and deadly calm, were:

"Haven't you got *any* sense of decency?"

"Bill, I'm sorry. Honestly, honestly I am. I never meant to do it. I just didn't think, that's all. When I walked out of that office —"

He blinked at her. His hands, raised for a gesture, stopped at his forehead.

"What office?" he demanded.

"The War Office, of course."

"The War Office? What about it?"

"Going out and leaving you like that. Bill, I apologize; and I'd never have done it in the world if I'd thought."

"I am not talking about that," said Bill. "I am asking you what you mean by parading your damned love affairs in front of everybody at Pineham?"

The desk chair was just behind Monica, and she sat down in it. She sat down slowly, groping for the back.

"I — I don't know what you're talking about."

"No? Well, *I* do. I have just met Frances Fleur at the main building." He pointed his finger at her. "Mind you," he continued, carefully defining his terms, "it is no concern whatever of mine. I am not a moralist. Oh, no. What you choose to do in your spare time is your affair and your affair alone. But at least you might have the elementary decency to keep quiet about it and refrain from boasting about it more than was necessary afterward."

He also had had his day of troubles. All afternoon, all the way out in the taxi, he had thought of nothing but Monica. Frances Fleur's information (imparted in all sincerity and with a sort of puzzled respect) had put the last touch to it. Just how mad he was even Monica could not guess. Dimly, with a misted eye, he discovered that there was someone else in the room: someone who sat on the couch and was looking at him in consternation over a newspaper.

"O'Brien," he said, "we will excuse you. It's all right now. Go on. Hurry."

"Yes, O'Brien," whispered Monica, also with deadly calm, "we will excuse you."

"There ain't nothing wrong, is there sir? What I

mean to say—"

"No, there is nothing wrong. Here's a quid. Here's two quid. For God's sake get out."

"Thanking you kindly, sir, but if there is anything I can—"

"No. Out."

"And now," whispered Monica, holding tightly to the edge of the desk, "is there anything further you would care to say to me? Of course, if you would really prefer to talk in front of a third person, as you have been doing, we can always call him back. Have you anything else to say to me?"

"Yes, madam, I have. It is this. Such singular talents as yours are wasted in a small country like England. They should be put at the service of your country. Why don't you go over to France and team up with Mademoiselle from Armentières? Then at least you would be doing something toward helping win the war."

This was where Monica slapped his face.

It was difficult for her to see it, but she caught the side of his cheek a stinger with her open hand. He laughed. The late Lord Byron, brooding in lonely grandeur among Alpine crags, never fetched up such cynical laughter as Bill Cartwright thought he was producing then.

"Ha ha ha," he said. "Ha ha ha ha ha. Exactly right. Exactly what I should have expected. Maidenly virtue, outraged, adopts its traditional reprisal. I am not impressed. I am not even amused. There is the other cheek. Why don't you hit that?"

Monica did, with a truly memorable wallop.

Now it was never afterward clear to Bill exactly

how the next part of it began, or why he came to do it. It was perhaps caused by a feeling that if he did not kiss the girl, then and there, he might do her real violence of an even more unpalatable sort. But this was an afterthought: unreliable.

What he does remember is that he put his arms around Monica and began kissing her with a vigor which would have interested the professional eye of a film director. "Began kissing" is not the right term. It suggests something interrupted; and this process, once Bill had got his grip firmly, was not interrupted.

This surprised him enough. What surprised him more was that after the first few seconds, during which there were fierce muttering sounds and (attempted) violent shakes of the head from Monica, she stopped resisting and began to kiss him in return. She was very warm to the touch, and the crooks of her arms closed round his neck and pressed there. This went on for some time; and the interlude was chaotic.

"Look here," he said, presently, disengaging himself in a dazed manner and conscious of the inadequacy of words; "look here: what I mean is, I love you."

"Well, why couldn't you *s-say* so?"

"How the hell could I say so when every time I tried to say so you jumped down my throat? I beg your pardon: that is a bad choice of phrase. What I mean is—"

"Bill Cartwright, aren't you *ever* serious?"

"Serious?" he roared. He was staggered. "What do you think I am now? I've never been as serious in my grim life. There is no mirth in me. I could not even raise the ghost of a chuckle if I saw General Goering slip on a banana-peel with all his medals fastened on loose. I am balmy. I love you. The question is, do you happen to have any lurking fondness for me?"

"No. I hate you," said Monica.

She demonstrated her hatred for several minutes more.

"I've been in love with you," continued Bill, "for a long time."

"How long?"

"Well, for a long time."

"Yes, but *how* long? Since when?"

"Since I met you in Tom's office."

"You mean when you said my book was lousy?"

"Angel-face, if you insist on bringing that up—"

"Do you still think it's lousy?"

"Yes."

"Well, maybe it is," said Monica, dreamily and comfortable. "I expect it is, after all, you know. I don't think I mind much now."

Whereupon Bill, in the wildness of true love, threw principle overboard and watched it drown without a groan. "It's nothing of the kind," he declared. "It's a fine book, a thundering fine novel—I mean that!— and anyone who says it isn't shall answer to me with broadswords. It's great stuff, Monica. I ought to know. I've been doing it for the screen."

"Bill, *darling*. Do you honestly mean that?"

"I do," he swore, and was beginning seriously to believe this himself. "It was simply that I got off on the wrong foot with you, that's all, and never put myself right. I was in the wrong mood, don't you see? It was lunch. I had a rotten lunch; some devilish concoction; lamb-chops and pineap . . ."

He paused.

The present is always there, to pop the unpleasant thought into your head. Something, even in a haze, is always ready to remind you of the unpaid bill and the little green goblin.

Lamb-chops and pineapple suggested Tilly Parsons; and Tilly Parsons suggested things he did not like to think about. Even while he held Monica tightly, he glanced toward Tilly's office. Tilly was standing at the open door, looking at them.

"Honey—" said Tilly.

Her voice was hoarse. She looked as though she had been crying.

Bill felt Monica's whole body stiffen in his arms; he felt a current of suspicion from her, as palpably as the body gives out heat. Monica jerked loose from him, moving backward and putting up a hand to her disheveled hair.

Tilly made a flapping sort of gesture. "Don't worry, honey," she said, not without bitterness. "I'm not going to bother you. I've got my last sequence to finish, and then I'm through. Only—I'm out of Chesters." Her tone was petulant. "Somebody's always swiping my Chesters. Isn't there a stray Chester in here some place, honey?"

"I'm sorry. There aren't any."

"But I'm always leaving them around, honey. Are you sure there isn't?"

"Quite sure. The only cigarettes here are the kind I smoke. You're welcome to them, if you like."

"But they're English! I can't smoke English cigarettes. Bill—no, you only smoke a pipe." Tilly was almost wailing. "Oh, Judas, I suppose they're better than nothing. I've got to smoke. Do you mind if I take one, honey?"

"Not at all. Help yourself."

Tilly went over to the desk. She opened the red leather box and took a cigarette. Even in the midst of doubt and black uncertainty, Bill Cartwright could not help feeling a twinge of pity for her. Tilly looked old and beaten. Her flabby hands trembled on the red lid of the box.

"Look, Bill," she said suddenly. "Monica thinks I did something. I think maybe you think so too, by the way you're looking at me. Well, I didn't. Wait, now! I'm not going to bust in on you." She put the cigarette into her mouth and lit it. "You two love each other. You're swell kids, and I'm glad. That's all."

She left them not without dignity; she closed the door, but she did not slam it. The black doubt grew still more confused in Bill's mind. Monica ran to him, and he put his arm around her.

"Why did you tell Frances Fleur to tell me not to be alone with her?" Monica demanded in a whisper.

"Because it was her voice—oh, I'm hanged if I know whether it was!"

"And she wrote those letters."

He whirled round. "Are you sure of that?"

Monica opened the drawer of the desk. She took out the manuscript-sheet and the letter; she held them out to him; and her fingers trembled.

"Here it is," Monica muttered. "She wrote the letters—only, as you say, I'm hanged if I know whether she did."

It appeared to be all up now. He spread out the two sheets on the desk. Though he was no handwriting expert, the similarity could escape nobody. He felt a dull wave go over his brain.

"Poor old Tilly!" he said.

"Why do you say poor old Tilly?"

"Because it's all wrong somehow, my dear. Even if Tilly did write this: even if she did yell outside the window: I've got an obstinate idea she did it for a good reason, which wasn't to hurt you. I can't quite believe it even when I see the proof. Wait; I've got a magnifying glass in my room. We'll have another look."

He went and brought the glass. His movements were automatic. He was still dazed with the fact that Monica was in love with him. He wanted to make some brilliant deduction. He held the glass over the words—and he was interrupted by a scream.

It was a scream, in Tilly's rasping voice, which started out strongly but ended in a choke and a cough. There was a heavy bumping sound, as of someone jumping or tramping on the floor. A chair was knocked over. Bill Cartwright ran for the door, but Tilly clawed it open before him.

Tilly was holding out the cigarette at arm's length, trying to look at it. But her eyes were out of focus. With her other hand she caught and pawed at the jamb of the door, so that the red nails left scratches in the paint. On her face was exactly the expression of a boy who tries to smoke his first pipe: stupid, perspiring, ill. Round her the burning tobacco was exuding an odor of which Bill caught a whiff, but only a whiff.

"It's *poisoned*," Tilly screeched at them. "this fag you gave me: it's *poisoned*. You want to kill me. You—"

Frantically she flung the cigarette at Monica. It struck the desk and fell on the linoleum, scattering fiery flakes. The breath sobbed and died in Tilly's lungs. Pressing her hands to her throat, she tried to lean up against the door, looking merely startled and scared, before she slid down in a bundle to the floor.

4

"Get back!" said Bill. "Get away, I tell you!"

He did not mean Monica's run toward the limp figure by the door. He meant her first instinctive gesture toward the cigarette, which was sending up a curl of thick and faintly sweetish smoke. He pulled Monica out of the way, and kicked the cigarette across the room. He blew into the air, fanning it with his hands. As though a shutter had clicked open in his mind, he saw the design now.

"But what—why—?"

"Because it was meant for you. It was certain to get you. Tilly won't smoke English cigarettes. I smoke only a pipe. Tom Hackett, the only other one of the gang in this building, doesn't smoke at all. Only: Tilly did."

"But how do you know? And what's in it?"

"What's in it is belladonna. It's one of the few poisons that can be turned into a deadly gas without any trouble or knowledge needed, by soaking tobacco in the liquid." His throat was dry. He went to Tilly and bent over her.

She was dying.

"And I know," he added in a frenzy, "because the swine has done it again. I've got a whole sheaf of notes on the stuff in my desk."

XII

The emergency dressing-station at Pineham opens off the big concrete hall outside the sound-stages. This hall was now nakedly lighted, and looked more than ever like the inside of an airport. The doctor came out and closed the door.

"This is all we want to know," said Bill. "Has she got any chance at all?"

His voice went up in echoes from the roof; and, in echoes, the doctor talked back at him.

"So little," said the latter, "that I shouldn't hope for anything. That stuff, when it's swallowed, is fairly slow. Unless it's a very big dose you can catch it in time. But taken through the lungs straight into the blood in the form of a gas — well, you saw how rapidly the symptoms came on. Hope for the best; but say your prayers."

"What have you done?"

"Hot coffee and injections of pilocarpine. The coffee, that is, if we can get her to drink it. She is delirious, and talking about somebody forging a check and some letters." The doctor looked very hard at Bill and

Monica. "I suppose you know this will have to be reported to the police?"

"To the police?" repeated Bill. His voice thundered back at him; he cleared his throat, and controlled himself. "That's the one thing I want most to see done. If only we had a capable officer here; if only we did! But no: it'll be nothing but fool, fool, fool, until something happens again."

Monica plucked at his sleeve. "But, Bill. I've just remembered. There is somebody here. A Scotland Yard man."

"A what?"

"A Scotland Yard man. His name is," she searched her memory, "Masters, I think."

"Masters here? Where is he?"

"With somebody named Mr. Marshlake. And the rest of them. At least, he was here a while ago. I don't know where he is now."

Even now it was difficult to realize that life had been turned upside down, and that Tilly Parsons lay choking her life out of belladonna poisoning only a few feet away. They had lost as little time as possible. They had brought her up from the Old Building in Bill's car, which he never took to town and kept conveniently parked there. How long Tilly would last depended on the amount of poison the murderer had tucked so carefully into a cigarette intended for Monica Stanton.

Monica's speculation as to Chief Inspector Master's whereabouts, however, was not long in being answered. Even as the name was spoken, a figure familiar to Bill Cartwright appeared from the glass corridor to the main building, glanced left and right, and saw them. Masters had a magisterial walk. But even at a distance his eye looked wicked. Bland as a card-sharper, the grizzled hair carefully brushed to hide the bald spot, he carried his hat cradled over his arm, and advanced upon them like a galleon under full sail.

"Ah, sir," he said grimly.

"Chief Inspector," said Bill, "allow me to shake your hand. You were never, anywhere or at any time, more welcome. But what in blazes are you doing here?"

"That's as may be, sir," returned Masters, with a dark look. "The point is that I am here, though without any authority whatever, at the instigation of a certain party whom I will not name" — he was in his worst magisterial mood — *"and* without so much as by-your-leave of the Buckinghamshire police."

"Meaning what?"

"Meaning, sir, that a few minutes ago I, and some others, heard someone run through here shouting that a lady named Miss Parsons had been murdered. Is that correct?"

"I'm afraid it is."

Masters compressed his lips.

"Oh, ah. Just so. I also learn, from conversations with certain other parties upstairs, that there's been a sort of reign of terror going on here. And that two attempts have already been made on the life of . . . ah . . . this young lady, maybe?"

"Yes. Chief Inspector Masters: Miss Stanton."

"How do you do, miss?" He turned again to Bill. "Now I don't mind telling you, sir, that this is a pretty serious business. Why wasn't it told to the police?"

"It was."

"Oh?"

"Yes. If you remember, I told you all about it a

fortnight ago. And you said it was probably a practical joke. You said it would be criminal to bother anybody with it at a time like this."

Masters changed color.

"Officially reported, sir. Very different thing. Now, will you just tell me what happened here tonight, and no funny business about it?"

Bill told him. At the end of it Masters glanced for confirmation at the doctor, who nodded.

"Oh, ah. I see. So you think someone put this hocused cigarette into the box on the table, knowing that sooner or later this young lady would get it, because nobody else there used her kind of tobacco?"

"Of course. And it could have been done by anybody or at any time. The box is always there. The cigarette may have been put there days ago."

This was the point at which Monica opened her mouth to protest. She visualized, with sharp vividness, every event of that day; she followed, in clear colors, every move she had made. But for the moment she kept it to herself.

"And this cigarette, sir. Have you got it?"

Bill shifted. "Well, no. I — "

"You haven't got it?"

"To tell the truth, Chief Inspector, I forgot all about the infernal thing. The last I saw of it, it was lying on the floor where I kicked it."

"The cigarette, sir, is evidence. But if there's somebody hanging about here, as seems probable, it may not be evidence much longer. Lummy, *I've* walked into a mess, and I know whose fault it is." He looked thoughtful. "At the same time, most of the people who seem to be concerned in this are safely upstairs in Mr.

Marshlake's office. Hurrum! That's to the good, anyhow."

"Who are up there?" asked Bill sharply.

"A Mr. Hackett, a Mr. Fisk, and a Miss Fleur."

Something had been on Monica's mind, nagging, for quite a while.

"There's something awfully queer about it, then," she burst out. Then she stopped, reddening.

"Yes, miss?" prompted Masters softly.

"I didn't mean that. It's nothing."

"Might as well get it off your chest, miss." The chief inspector's tone was insinuating. "We never know, do we?"

"Well, it's about Frances Fleur. When she left me—which was before seven o'clock—she said she was going straight into town to meet her husband. Then, at well past seven o'clock, she met Bill here in the grounds and told him some things." This was what rankled, though Monica hurried over it. "Now, at eight o'clock, you say she's been upstairs talking to you."

It was Bill who answered.

"That's all right," he assured her, with equal haste. "I left Gagern in town waiting for her. I—er—happened to run into him there. When I came back here, and my taxi was going by the door of the main building, I saw her standing on the steps. It was a quarter past seven; not quite dark even though all the windows were blacked out. I let my cab go and asked her whether she'd delivered my message to Miss Stanton." (He was now speaking loudly to Masters.) "I also told her she'd catch it from Gagern for being late. She said she'd decided not to go to town after all, and had phoned Gagern to tell him so. She also told me about a little unimportant gossip, Chief Inspector: which I never believed for a second, though I may have made some foolish joke about it afterward."

"Now, now, sir, there's no call to shout. I can hear you."

Bill broke off, guilty but even more worried.

"And yet there's still something odd about it," he muttered. He remembered Frances Fleur standing on the white steps under strengthening starlight, with the ghostly buildings of Pineham around her. "Frances didn't say anything about *you* being here, Chief Inspector. That is, if she knew?"

"She knew," Monica informed him.

(Yes, and Masters's manner was distinctly odd too.)

"Well, sir, it's just possible she didn't want that news spread about," chuckled Masters. "People don't, you know. Not with coppers. Anyway, she's certainly been with me, and a few others too, since twenty minutes past seven. A very attractive lady, that. Oh, ah. Ve-ery attractive."

He mused. But he had an ear like a microphone. He turned to Monica.

"I-beg-pardon, miss? What was that you just said about 'unimportant gossip'?"

"Nothing. I was only talking to myself."

"Ah? I thought it might be important."

"Chief Inspector," Bill said slowly, "I don't know what you're doing here; and you don't seem inclined to be communicative. I can only say that, if you've got no legal authority, you must have remarkable powers of conversation to keep that whole crowd from their dinners until eight o'clock."

"Well, sir, I don't know that it's *my* remarkable

powers of conversation keeping them from their dinners. Or me from my dinner either, if it comes to that. I'd take it as a great favor, though, if you and the lady would just come with me. . . . You'll be standing by, Doctor?"

"Yes. Ring through if you want me."

Masters led them back through the glass-enclosed passage to the main entrance. He led them up a staircase to a gallery, off which opened many little offices. He showed them into one of these offices.

Inside, fat and patient and malignant as the Evil One, sat Sir Henry Merrivale.

2

H.M. sat by a shiny desk on which there was one of those box-telephones, for inter-office communication, of the sort where you throw a switch and shout. This seemed to intrigue him immensely. But there was a worried look about his forehead.

"So you found 'em," he said.

"I found them," agreed Masters. "And—trouble happened sooner than you said it would. Miss Parsons got a poisoned cigarette out of a box on this young lady's desk. Miss Stanton, Sir Henry Merrivale."

H.M. lumbered to his feet, ducked his bald head gravely, and sat down again.

"So," he muttered. "Is she . . .?"

"Probably."

"And so," interposed Bill Cartwright, "you decided to come and lend us a hand after all?"

"I'm interested in that missing film," howled H.M. "That's all I'm interested in. Only, I got a conscience. I can't stand by and see somebody headed straight for the rollin' mill without doing anything about it." His eyes fixed on Monica. Then they moved toward the door to the communicating office, behind which there was a murmur of voices.

"I've seen the dramatis personae," he went on. "I had some questions I wanted to ask all of 'em. Particularly Miss Fleur."

"Yes," said Masters, "and fine questions they were! Begging your pardon, miss: the first question he asked her was whether, when they showed her in a bathtub on the screen, it was a fake or the real thing."

H.M. sniffed.

"Well, I was curious. All my life, mostly, I've been wantin' to visit a film studio. And, now that I do get a reasonable excuse to look at one, it's as black as a coal cellar. Y'know, Masters, I'm potentially a very fine actor myself. I've always thought I could play Richard the Third."

"You?"

"I'd like to know why not," roared H.M., stung to the soul. "It was my great ambition in the old days. I told you I was a pal of Henry Irving. I wasn't bald then; I was a fine figger of a man. I was always goin' on at him to let me play Richard the Third."

"Oh, ah? And did he?"

"Well, no," admitted H.M. grudgingly. "Not exactly. He said, 'My dear sir, nothing would afford me greater pleasure than to allow you to play Richard the Third. But candidly, sir, if I were to allow you to play Richard the Third, or, in fact, do anything except carry a spear and keep quiet, I should have the Lyceum pulled stone from stone under me.' That's all the artistic appreciation *he* had. And, with regard to artistic appreciation, we seem to have a lot of it in this place. A poisoned cigarette, hey? Poisoned with what?"

"Belladonna," said Bill.

"Belladonna. Judgin' by your expression, I suppose that was your bright idea too?"

"Don't rub it in." He felt badly enough as it was. Everywhere he seemed to see Tilly's face. "I made some notes on belladonna, yes; but the poisoned cigarette was only one of them. I had the notes in my desk, yes. But every time you think of writing a story you don't think somebody will . . ."

It was too baffling to explain. He wanted to hit out at the air.

"Besides, the murderer needn't have got the idea from me. I didn't invent it. It was done in real life. One of the victims in the Mold case in 1923 was killed by a cigar impregnated with belladonna."*

"Easy, son. Just tell me what happened. Wait!"

Painfully moving, H.M. reached out and touched the switch of the box-telephone.

"That thing was on before," he said softly. "It's off now. I'm goin' to switch it on again; and I want you to know that everything you say will be heard by an

---

*Should anyone care to check up on William Cartwright's facts, an account of this case is in *Poison Mysteries Unsolved,* by C.J.S. Thompson, M.B.E., Ph.D., with a foreword by Gerald Roche Lynch (Hutchinson & Co., 1937) p. 275.

interested group in the next room. So let's have it hot and strong. Ready?" He clicked the switch.

Monica conquered her aversion.

"Please!" she said. "Before you go any further, there's something you ought to know. I can tell you the only time the cigarette could have been put into that box."

The feeling caused by her first sight of H.M. had been one of incredulous astonishment. Whatever she had expected him to look like, she had not expected him to look like that. And yet there was something about him: something.

Besides, the effect of this announcement on her listeners was electrical. H.M. stretched out his hand as though to cut off the switch of the listening-box again; but, after exchanging a glance with Masters, he kept it. Monica's knowledge that she was talking to people in another room only strengthened her determination.

She told her story in detail, including the receipt of the third anonymous letter and Tilly's denial of it. But before she had finished H.M. interrupted her. His exchange of glances with Masters had been growing more curious.

"Stop a bit," he urged, rubbing his chin. "Let's see if I've got this straight. You bought a box of fifty cigarettes at the tobacconist's in Marylebone Street station just before you took the train?"

"Yes."

Chief Inspector Masters whistled through his teeth.

"Which," Masters pointed out, "disposes of any idea that the poisoned cigarette was in the original fifty. That's to say, sir, nobody would shove a poisoned cigarette in a box at the railway station just in the hope that Miss Stanton would come along and buy it."

"Be quiet, Masters," said H.M., putting his thick hands on his knees and bending forward. "Now, then. You put the original fifty into your handbag?"

"Yes."

"And that bag, you say, wasn't out of your hands from the moment you put the cigarettes in it until the time you turned 'em out into the red leather box?"

"No, it wasn't." Monica could say this firmly. "Even when I went into Tilly's room for a minute or two when I came back, I carried the handbag with me."

H.M. implored her. "Now for the love of Esau think hard here. Before you put the cigarettes into the leather box, was that box empty?"

"Yes, it was."

"Positive of that, now? There couldn't have been a stray cigarette inside?"

"I'm absolutely positive it was empty. I even turned it upside down to shake out some loose tobacco-crumbs."

"And after you dumped the cigarettes into the box, you didn't leave the room at any time?"

"No, not once."

Masters, with a boiled blue eye turned strangely on her, chewed at his lower lip. "It'd seem," he said to H.M., "it'd seem that our man is coming right out in the open. Somebody's got a beautiful nerve. Some-body slipped that poisoned fag into the box smack under this young lady's eyes. It ought to be easy now. — Miss, who was in the room between the time you put the cigarettes into the box and the time Miss Parsons got the poisoned one?"

Monica shut her eyes.

"Well, there was Tilly herself, of course . . ."

"Who else?" demanded H.M.

"Then there was Bill. But he didn't do it; and anyway—" She stopped.

"Anyway, what?"

"Please, never mind that! We were discussing personal matters. We were—"

Bill leaned across with decision, threw the switch which cut off the listening-box, and completed the sentence for her.

"Canoodling," he said. "It was fine. I was asking her to marry me."

"You never did!"

"Well, will you?"

"Yes."

"All right, then," said Bill, and threw the switch back again.

He rather expected H.M. to hit the ceiling about this, but H.M. merely sat and stared fishily at Monica. Yet of all the refined forms of torture he could have devised for people listening in another room, this sudden break-and-return was perhaps the most effective.

"Then," prompted H.M., "excluding this young feller, who else was there?"

"A man called O'Brien. But he was never anywhere near the desk. He sat on the couch and stayed there."

"Uh-huh. Go on."

"The only others were Miss Fleur, Mr. Hackett, and Mr. Fisk."

"So? So any of those three could have done it?"

As though on a colored cinema film itself, the scene was unrolling to Monica: even to the fact that she could stop the film and study it whenever she liked.

Faces returned. Voices returned, and gestures, and inflections.

"No," she replied promptly.

"What do you mean, no?"

"I mean that there was one of them who definitely couldn't have done it."

"Which one?" asked H.M. Very deliberately he reached out and pressed the switch, cutting off the connection.

"Mr. Hackett. I remember everything he did. He walked over and stood in front of me. He wasn't in there for very long, and he wasn't a yard away from me the whole time."

Again H.M. exchanged a glance with the chief inspector.

"What about the other two?"

"Miss Fleur was there a longer time. She did go to the desk, and I remember she did put her hand on top of the box." Then the stark absurdity of this struck Monica; she giggled rather than laughed at the idea of the glamorous Miss Fleur being a poisoner. "But I didn't see her open the box," Monica added.

"So. What about the other one, the director?"

Monica hesitated.

"He was sitting on the desk for a very few minutes. I didn't notice what he was doing, except that he seemed to be playing with a paper-knife."

"Was he near the box?"

"He was within reach of it, anyway."

"So you'd say" — there was a sharp metallic *plop* as again H.M. pressed the switch to open the connection to the other room — "you'd say that was the person likeliest to have slipped the cigarette into the box?"

Monica's head ached. The sharp little noise of the switch was beginning to affect her own nerves.

"I — I don't know. It seems incredible. But then anybody seems incredible. I don't know."

"Nobody else came into the room at any time?"

"Nobody."

"Or could have sneaked in?"

"Good heavens, no!"

"Now, about these anonymous letters. Have you kept 'em all?"

"Yes. I haven't got the first two here, but the third is down in my desk at the Old Building now."

"Tilly Parsons denied having written them. Hey?"

"Yes."

"Do you think she did?"

(*Plop* went the switch again.)

"I don't know," Monica answered helplessly. "If she did" — she glanced at Bill — "I think Tilly had some good reason for doing it. I don't want Tilly to die. You mustn't let her die."

It was Chief Inspector Masters who interposed here. Masters, pinching at his under-lip, had been prowling back and forth in the little office, and shaking his head in a doubtful way.

"Excuse me, sir," he interposed, "but are you *sure* you're on the right track with what you think? Just offhand I'd say that this business of the Parsons woman has all the ear-marks of suicide. Get Mr. Cartwright to tell you about it. What she said and did, and how she behaved at the time. Suppose she put the poisoned fag in the box herself; and then got a change of heart and took it herself?"

H.M. looked steadily at Monica. "Go on," he said.

217

"Round up your story. Finish it off."

As Monica did so, with the connection open between the offices, Masters looked more doubtful, but H.M. only more intent: with a groping expression which grew distinctly disturbing.

"These domestic details," he mumbled. "They're very fascinatin'. Also—but I want to see that for myself. Now tell me. Frances Fleur, and these two fellers Hackett and Fisk, were all in your office together. Do you remember what time they left?"

Monica considered.

"It was well before seven o'clock. I should say twenty or twenty-five minutes to seven."

"Did they leave together?"

"No. Miss Fleur went on ahead, and the other two stopped to talk to Tilly in her office."

"Did they now? How long were they with her?"

"Not very long. They were in a hurry to come up and see you—or, rather, Chief Inspector Masters. They didn't know you were here. They were only in Tilly's room between five and ten minutes. Then they went out, and Tilly walked to the front door with them."

Masters frowned.

"That'd be about right, sir," he pointed out to H.M. "They met us up here at ten minutes to seven, though Miss Fleur didn't join us until twenty past. What about it?"

H.M. silenced him with a fierce gesture. "And then what?"

"Then Tilly tried to come into my room, and wanted me to join her. But I wouldn't, and O'Brien was there, so she slammed the door and went back into her office."

H.M. pointed a big finger toward Bill. "Yes. And what time did *he* arrive?"

"Twenty minutes past seven. I'm sure of that."

"So. And how long after this did the Parsons woman come in and get the poisoned cigarette?"

"I — I'm not sure."

Bill cleared his throat. "Nor am I," he said, "in much of a position accurately to tell the time there. My impression was that it was about seven-thirty."

"Near enough," Monica acknowledged.

H.M. got to his feet.

"Come with me, all of you," he said. "I've got something I'd rather like to show you."

XIII

"That's it," said Bill.

He pointed to the half-smoked cigarette, which still lay along the baseboard where he had kicked it.

The four of them stood in Monica's office. They had come down to the Old Building in Bill's car, but only after H.M. and Masters had gone into a long conference with Hackett, Fisk, and Frances Fleur. It was a conference to which Monica and Bill were not admitted; they were compelled to kick their heels and fume in an outer room. Yet, curiously enough, the conference seemed to have no noise of animosity in it. On the contrary, they could have sworn they once heard a shout of jubilation from Thomas Hackett.

H.M. planted himself in the middle of the office. He was wearing a bowler hat. Due to a complaint from the Secretary for War that H.M.'s usual headgear was a disgrace to Whitehall in war time, he had been persuaded to replace it with a new bowler: neat, not gaudy. Yet the spectacle of H.M. in a bowler hat is one which has to be seen to be believed.

This article ornamented—let us be charitable—his

head as he peered round, sniffing the air. He lumbered over to where the cigarette lay; he bent over, and with infinite labor picked it up. He smelt it.

"This is the little joker, right enough," he said. "have a whiff, Masters."

The chief inspector studied it, and scowled uneasily.

"Oh, ah. But see, here, sir: how was it done? This looks like an ordinary Player's cigarette. Got the name printed on the unsmoked end, and everything. If the murderer soaked his tobacco in a solution of belladonna and then rolled it, he did a very neat job. It's not so easy to roll a cigarette so it looks like a machine-made one."

"I can tell you how to do that," said Bill. "Tilly told me."

Masters swung round sharply. "Miss Parsons told you?"

"Yes. It seems that in New York you can buy little machines for rolling cigarettes at any drugstore. The state recently put a two-cent tax on cigarettes and a number of people have taken to rolling their own. If you used English tobacco and a Player's cigarette-paper (though I don't know where you'd get that) you could make a perfect counterfeit. Tilly has one of the little gadgets herself."

The chief inspector's brow darkened with suspicion.

"Is that so, now?" he mused, in a sinister voice. "So the lady's got one herself, has she?"

H.M. was not impressed.

"Oh, Masters, my son!" he said wearily. "Stop goin' off the deep end again! I can tell you an easier way than that. Just dip half of the cigarette into your solution, and let it dry. The color of the paper will be a bit different afterward, but not noticeably. Bella-donna — don't you remember we ran into its derivative, atropine, in the Felix Haye case?* — is a colorless liquid. The maker's name proves it, son."

"Not to me it doesn't," snapped Masters. "Just you look here, sir."

He went to the red leather box on the desk, and tapped it.

"Presumably," he went on, "there was only one poisoned fag in here. That's to say, it isn't likely the murderer would have shoved in a whole handful. Anyway, we can find out by counting them. *But*" — he raised a finger impressively — "there was one doctored cigarette and fifty harmless ones. And Miss Parsons gets the doctored one first crack out of the box. No, sir. That's not reasonable: unless she knew which one it was. And I'll just lay you a little bet she did."

H.M. eyed him curiously.

"So you see somethin' fishy about it too?" he inquired. "Uh-huh. Just a minute."

In an absent-minded way he went to the door of Tilly's office, opened it, and blinked at the room inside. The light was still on; a faint odor of the cigarette still remained. The room was, as usual, strewn with crumpled papers. A cup of now-cold coffee stood on the desk beside the standing ashtray.

H.M. lumbered over. He looked at the ashtray, its edges scarred with burns. He examined the cup of coffee. Then he went wandering round the room

*Cf. *Death in Five Boxes,* William Morrow & Co., New York, 1938.

inspecting everything.

"I say," he called out. They could not see his face. "Was the gal drinkin' coffee just before the poison got her?"

Masters was after this like a terrier.

"Hold on, sir! What's the game? Is there a double-cross in this? Are you trying to tell us she might have got the poison in the coffee?"

"No," said H.M. "The poison was in the cigarette all right." Still without looking round at them, he put his hands up to his temples and pressed them there. "I was askin' a plain question, and I'd like a plain answer. Was she drinking coffee when the poison got her?"

Monica and Bill exchanged glances.

"I don't remember," Monica answered. "I don't even remember looking in there. I expect she was, though. She drank coffee all day."

"Yes," said H.M. "You mentioned that before That's the whole sad, sweet story: she drank coffee all day."

H.M. turned round. His face had a queer look which was a good deal more sinister than Masters's darkest scowl.

"Look here," he said to Monica. "Just start in again, slowly, and tell me everything that happened to you since the time you ditched this feller at the War Office today. You be like the old detective stories: don't leave *anything* out, no matter how unimportant it seems. For the love of Esau, think!"

"But there's nothing I haven't told you," Monica protested. "Except, of course—"

"Except what?"

"Except that I met Jimmy, the page-boy, on the way

down here." She explained this, and to her astonishment H.M. listened with grim attention. "That's all," she concluded, "though I shouldn't put any great reliance on what he says. He also told me Miss Fleur was carrying a beer bottle when he met her on the Eighteen-eighty-two set just before . . ."

Monica stopped, somewhat frightened. Her three listeners whirled round to her.

"A beer bottle," muttered Chief Inspector Masters. "Gawdlummy-charley!"

"Yes, but what about it?"

"The acid that was poured at you," said Bill, "was poured out of a beer bottle. I found it upstairs at the doctor's house, and took it along to the War Office in my brief-case today."

There was no time to comment on this. From outside there was the noise of a rush on the Old Building, as though it were being attacked. Thomas Hackett, a hooded electric torch in his hand, burst in on them. Behind him stumbled Howard Fisk, adjusting his pince-nez.

"It's all right," the producer said. "We don't need the police. I'm not a praying man, but, by George! I could fire away with a couple of prayers now. Tilly's up."

H.M. stared at him, and seemed to be swallowing a prayer himself.

"Up? Take it easy, son. You mean it's all up with her?"

"I mean she's sitting up," shouted Mr. Hackett. He was so excited that the torch slid out of his hand and smashed on the floor. "The doctor gave her two injections of some stuff called pilocarpine, and she sat up and clouted him one. She's up there drinking brandy

224

and swearing a blue streak. The doctor nearly fainted. He says she must have a constitution like a goat: he says he'd back her to swallow six tin cans and a pint of liquid concrete without turning a hair. She's not going to die: do you understand that?"

Mr. Hackett cleared his throat. He got out a handkerchief and wiped his forehead. With a kind of shudder, as though he were so relieved that it almost choked him, he sat down on the couch. Howard Fisk was looking rather white.

"It is a relief," the director conceded in his soft voice. "It is a great relief. After that ingenious game of tease-the-listener you played on us, Sir Henry, it is something to know that none of us has murder on his conscience. At the same time, I have a complaint to make. What have you done to poor old Frances?"

"Frances?" said H.M.

The director took two steps forward.

"Yes, Frances. If I were you I should take some care. Gagern is back from town, and he is looking for you. I shouldn't be surprised if you were challenged to a duel with the *schlager*. What did you say to her, in that private interview you had? She went away crying. I know, because I saw her. I didn't even know she could cry. For five years I've been trying to make her do it in films, and I can't. What did you say to her?"

H.M.'s eyes were shaded by his forehead under the remarkable bowler hat.

"I told her a few home truths," he said, rather dully. "Sit down, son."

"Home truths? You mean . . ."

The director's mouth worked. He looked at Mr. Hackett. He did not seem to know what to do with his large-knuckled hands.

"I said sit down, son."

Yet, Monica thought, there were some grounds for Mr. Fisk's uneasiness. Kurt von Gagern, who arrived just then, was in no frame of mind to be trusted. He breathed noisily through his nose, which stood out reddish and as though detached from his face. Under the brim of his rakish soft hat, which shaded eyes watery from cold, the look he directed at H.M. could not be called respectful.

"Where," he said, "is my wife? What have you done with my wife?"

"She's all right," H.M. assured him. "She's maybe a little bit upset over bein' asked some inconvenient questions about a beer bottle and three anonymous letters; but I got no doubt she'll get over it."

"A beer bottle and three anonymous letters? What exactly do you mean?"

"If you'll all make yourselves comfortable," said H.M., "I'll tell you. We'd better have this out here and now."

An abrupt silence, with something of an unpleasantly eerie quality in it, set them all looking at each other. H.M. went into Tilly's room and returned with two chairs. He made Monica sit down in one of these, facing the others, as though she were a school pupil on exhibition. He himself sat down in the chair beside the desk.

Removing his bowler hat, he put it down carefully. He picked up the red leather box, and drew it over so that everybody could see it. Then, with the greatest deliberation, he drew a black pipe and an oilskin to-bacco-pouch from the pocket of his baggy coat. Still deliberately, he unscrewed the pipe and blew down the stem. His puffed cheeks and cross-eyed concentration, under the light which Monica had shaded with a newspaper, gave him rather the appearance of an elderly Humpty Dumpty. He fitted the pipe together, filled it with a tobacco which tasted like the steel-wool that is used to clean kitchen sinks, and lighted it. The smoke curled up round his head, into the cone of the lamp.

"Masters," he continued, settling himself back at ease, "you made a thunderin' good suggestion a while ago." He reached out and tapped the lid of the leather box. "These cigarettes. Count 'em."

"Eh?"

"Turn 'em out and count 'em. Let us hear you count 'em."

Masters, frowning, opened the box and rolled the pile of cigarettes across the desk. He pushed them to one side in neat, swift batches, like a bank clerk.

"Four, eight, twelve, sixteen. Twenty, twenty-four, twenty-eight, thirty-two. Thirty-six, forty, forty-four, forty . . ." Masters stopped. His face grew more ruddy. He went back and began to count again; then he blinked at H.M.

"No, son," said H.M., who appeared to be deriving intense satisfaction from his pipe. "You didn't make any mistake. Now we can go ahead with a clear conscience, and know smackin' well we're right. The would-be murderer had an awful nasty break from the cussedness of things in general." He made a gesture toward Bill Cartwright. "*You* count 'em, son."

"See here —" began Thomas Hackett, running a finger round inside his collar.

Bill himself had for some minutes been conscious of

trouble ahead. But instead he wanted to laugh. The spectacle of Gagern, Fisk, and Hackett, sitting side by side on the couch and facing Monica, was not one that could be seen with a grave face. Yet his brain felt heavy and dull. He had counted the cigarettes twice before he realized what the total was.

"There's something wrong," he said, in a voice which blattered out with startling loudness. "There are only forty-nine cigarettes here."

Thomas Hackett jumped up, and sat down again.

"That's right, son," agreed H.M., waving a sticky cloud of smoke away from in front of his face. His ghoulish relish deepened. "Now, Joe—"

"I do not know whom you are calling Joe," said Gagern, his voice rather shrill.

"We'll consider it unsaid, then. Today," continued H.M., "you asked me six questions, which had to be answered before we could see daylight in this business. Uh-huh. If you'll just ask the same questions again, I'll try to answer 'em."

Gagern hesitated.

"I do not remember the order of the questions; but what they were I remember with a painful clarity. Very well. The first question is, who stole the film, and why?"

H.M. took the pipe out of his mouth.

"There never was any film stolen, son," he said.

If a small bomb had exploded under the sofa, there could not have been any more uproar.

"See here," said Mr. Hackett, again running his finger round inside his collar, and appealing to Masters. "I don't want to seem critical, Mr. Masters, but is your friend raving mad? Do you deny the film is gone?"

"I don't deny it's gone," said H.M. "All I said was: it wasn't stolen."

"Are you accusing me of stealing my own film?"

"What's the next question, son?"

"The next question," returned Gagern, after looking rather vacantly at the floor, "is: who put the acid in the water bottle on that set, and why?"

"Ah!" said H.M., with glee. "Now we're comin' to it. Answer: the same person who poured the acid down the speaking-tube, fired the revolver-shot, and prepared the poisoned cigarette. He put that acid in the water bottle to underline the fact, to set it yellin' before high heaven, that apparently there was a maniac loose and determined on sabotage. So he took ruddy good care to knock the water bottle over."

Hitherto Howard Fisk had not said anything. Nor did he say anything now. He sat stolid as a grandmother at a family reunion, his big hands folded in his lap; but the incredulous smile which went over his face answered for him.

Mr. Hackett was not so stolid.

"Are you going to take that lying down, Howard?" he demanded.

"Next question, son," said H.M.

"The next question," replied Gagern, "is one that most of us would rather have answered than anything else. What is the reason for the intense personal animosity which the—er—author of all this has shown toward Miss Stanton?"

H.M. drew a deep breath. "And the answer, son, is short and sweet. There never was the slightest animosity toward her."

"The man's mad," said Mr. Hackett, rather wildly. "He's clean off his chump. I didn't think so before, but I know it now. — You'll be telling us next that Miss Stanton was never attacked at all."

H.M. nodded.

"You're quite right, son," he agreed with profound seriousness. "She never was."

"Somebody," said the producer through his teeth, "tries to burn out her eyes with vitriol, fires a bullet straight at her, and slips a cigarette loaded with belladonna into a box on her desk. And yet you say she wasn't attacked?"

"Well" said H.M., examining the side of his pipe, and taking a reflective puff at it, "it depends on your definition of attack, and also the direction of the attack. First of all the would-be murderer was misled; and later he misled you all to a fare-ye-well. However, that's gettin' ahead of myself. Next question?"

"But all the next questions," said Gagern, "take care of that. Who twice attacked Miss Stanton, and why? Are all these things connected, and if so, how?"

"Ah!" said H.M.

He took a last puff at his pipe. He put it down carefully in the ashtray, and got to his feet. He lumbered over to the couch. The expression of his eye was not pleasant.

"They're all connected, son, in a way," he replied.

"In what way? And why?"

H.M. came closer. His own expression was almost maniacally pleased. Before anybody could move he had shot out his hand, laid hold of the necktie of Joe Collins, alias Kurt von Gagern, wrapped the necktie round his hand, and yanked the slight form halfway to its feet.

He said:

"Because, Joe, you're the little joker who's responsible for all this. You're the feller who poured the acid, fired the revolver shot, and have now just failed to kill with a poisoned cigarette the woman you married in Hollywood two years ago."

Then his voice roared out.

"And lemme tell you somethin' else, Joe. If you share the general belief that the old man is gettin' senile and dodderin' and ready for the House of Lords: if you think I didn't know the whole ruddy scheme was directed against Tilly Parsons to start with: then you better soak your head in cold water before you come round to me again with a song-and-dance about wantin' to join up in the service again. We may not be able to prove attempted murder on you, but you'll do time for bigamy just as soon as Tilly Parsons sets eyes on your handsome mug—and that's what you wanted to avoid all along, ain't it?"

Gagern did not reply. He could not, for the necktie was half strangling him. But his face was green, and a kind of bubbling squeal came from between his lips. When H.M. released him, he dropped with a boneless thud to the floor; and the tears in his eyes were more real than those caused by a ducking in the lake.

XIV

"Me?" said Tilly Parsons. "You couldn't kill me with a battle-axe. I'm raring to go. Got a Chester, somebody?"

Thus spoke Tilly two days later, in a fine mellow afternoon when these affairs ended — as they had begun — in the office of Mr. Thomas Hackett of Albion Films.

Mr. Hackett, a noble host, had provided cocktails to celebrate both the completion of *Spies at Sea* and the end of Joe Collins's meteoric career as a would-be murderer. It is true that Tilly still looked a trifle white round the gills, but she wore a dress whose colors could have been discerned by a blind man at a distance of thirty yards, and she was polishing off Old Fashioneds at a rate which made Mr. Hackett's own eyes stand out of his head.

Indeed, it gave signs of becoming, if somebody were not careful, a party. It was indecorous of Monica Stanton and Bill Cartwright to adjourn to the next office every ten minutes for the purpose of what Tilly called necking, though excusable. Mr. Howard Fisk was there, with his arm round a young actress whom he was grooming in several senses. Miss Frances Fleur—whose distress at the whole affair had lasted exactly twenty-four hours—drank (to the regret of everybody) orange juice.

But in the midst of them, perhaps prouder than he had ever been since the day he got James Answell acquitted on a murder charge at the Old Bailey,[*] sat Sir Henry Merrivale. You would never, of course, have guessed this. He kept up a steady and malignant glare which made Mr. Fisk's young actress jump out of her skin whenever he turned toward her. Yet he was happy: for he was going to have a screen-test as Richard the Third; and he had been provided with real armor and a helmet to play it in.

"Come on," said Tilly. "You know why you're here, Ancient Mariner. And you don't fool me with your glittering eye, either. Let's hear about it. Tell us how you tumbled to him when none of the rest of us did. Since it's all my fault, in a way, I want to hear about it."

"Are you sure you want to hear about it?" asked Howard Fisk quietly.

For a moment Tilly's face pinched up. Whether it was sentimentality, or alcohol, or real emotion, perhaps Tilly herself could not have said. But, after a spasm had gone over her face, she got out a handkerchief, wiped her eyes, and defiantly finished her cocktail.

---

[*]Cf. *The Judas Window,* William Morrow & Co., New York, 1938.

"You bet I want to hear about it," she retorted. "After all, if Frances can take it, *I can.* The little son of a so-and-so stung her worse than he stung me." She regarded Miss Fleur with real and frank curiosity. "How *did* he get round you, dearie?"

Miss Fleur, sipping orange juice, returned the curiosity with interest.

"That makes us rivals, doesn't it?" Miss Fleur asked, with slight surprise. "Fancy that." She laughed.

Tilly stiffened.

"And what," she inquired, "is so funny about that?"

"Nothing, dear."

"You mean I'm a hag?" asked Tilly, with candor. "Sure I am. I never thought the fellow married me for my boz-yew. But there's life in the old dame yet, dearie, and don't you forget it. After all, I'm not the betrayed woman in this business. You are."

Miss Fleur put down her glass. "Are you insinuating that I am a betrayed woman?"

"Oh, well, what's a little betrayal among friends?" said Tilly, broad-minded to the last. "Judas, if that's the worst that ever happens to me, I'll think I've got off lucky. As far as I'm concerned, the atrocities can start any time they want to. Which reminds me"—she turned to Monica and Bill—"that the way you two are carrying on is a public scandal. What would your Aunt Flossie say, if she could see you now? Foo! Shame on you! (Set 'em up again, Tommy, and don't spare the rye.)"

"Good old Aunt Flossie!" said Bill, taking Monica carefully into his lap, and kissing her.

"Terrible," said Tilly, absent-mindedly clucking her tongue. "Shocking. What was I saying? The old Ancient Mariner. Come on, honey. Tell us about it. What do you say?"

For some time H.M., sunk in a tense and brooding meditation, had chewed on a cigar and said no word. His faint, muttering voice reached them from afar.

" *'Now is the winter of our discontent,'* " whispered H.M., with a sudden semaphore gesture which upset Howard Fisk's glass, " *'made glorious summer by this sun of York. Now—'* "

"Sure, honey. It's swell: you'll lay 'em in the aisles. But what about paying some attention to us for a change?"

The ensuing scene was chaotic. Imprimis, H.M. did not like being addressed as the Ancient Mariner; and, secondly, he said he had artistic temperament and must not be interrupted while rehearsing his lines. He howled about ingratitude to such an extent that it took some minutes to soothe him down. When he did continue, it was with a sort of weary patience.

"Now looky here," he said. "The easiest way to straighten out this tangle is to let you straighten it out for yourselves, by rememberin' what happened. Then you'll see it with very little pushing from me."

He smoked for a time in silence. Then he peered over his spectacles, first at Monica and then at Thomas Hackett.

"I want you," he continued, "to sort of cast your minds back to the afternoon of August 23, and to this office—where it all started. You," he pointed to Monica, "and you," his finger moved to Hackett, "are sittin' here talking before young Cartwright comes in. Got that?"

"Yes," said Monica.

"Yes," said the producer.

"All right. And the telephone rings: remember? All right. Who is on the phone?"

"Kurt Gagern," replied Mr. Hackett. His face darkened. "Or Joe Collins. Or whatever his blasted name is."

H.M. peered at Monica. "I remember, because Mr. Hackett addressed him as Kurt. What about it?"

"He told you," continued H.M., turning to Hackett again, "about the acid being upset on the set. You said you didn't want to come over to the sound-stage for a minute or two. Now, why? Think! What else did you say?"

The producer's eyes narrowed. He stared at the telephone. Then, as though struck on the back of the head with enlightenment, he snapped his fingers.

"I said, *'The new writer has just arrived,'*" he answered.

2

"Exactly," said H.M. " 'The new writer has just arrived.' Now I want you to stop for a second and think of the lurid and appallin' significance of those words. I want you to think what they meant to the feller who was listening to them.

"What in blazes would they naturally mean? Ever since the middle of the month it had been decided that Tilly Parsons, the great scenario-writer, should come over from Hollywood to work on *Spies at Sea*. Nobody knew exactly when she was to get here: you didn't know it yourself. But she was expected. The thoughts of all you people, including Gagern (let's call him that) were exclusively and burningly concentrated on *Spies at Sea*. When Gagern heard over the phone that the new writer had arrived, what was he goin' to think? What would anybody have thought?"

H.M. paused.

He looked at Tilly.

"Now Gagern was already preparing for your arrival. He'd arranged that little comedy with the acid in the water bottle so that there would seem to be a maniac and a saboteur on the premises, and later— when you did arrive—it'd cause no stunned astonishment when acid was poured into your face to . . ."

Tilly was looking white. Monica herself did not feel well.

". . . to blind you," concluded H.M. "He was expert enough at changing his voice so that he could still escape detection provided there was no possibility of your seeing him.

"Y'see, there was no other way out. He couldn't run away. He was very merciful. He didn't want to kill you. He just wanted to blind you.

"As I say, he'd already prepared the way for this by his little trick with the water bottle. He'd timed this to take place several days to a week before your actual arrival. So it must have given him a whale of a shock to ring up here, reporting the acid being upset on the set, and to discover that Tilly Parsons—apparently—was already here. He had to work like lightning now, or he'd be caught. He was scared; but he wasn't at all surprised that Tilly Parsons had turned up so unexpectedly. Why should he be? Anybody who knew you would know that turnin' up unexpectedly would be exactly the sort of thing you would do.

"Now, what happened next? *You*"—here H.M. pointed to Thomas Hackett—"rushed over to the sound stage, leaving Monica Stanton with Bill Cartwright. Yes?"

"Yes," conceded Mr. Hackett.

"You told Cartwright to bring her over to the sound stage, didn't you? H'mf, yes. Now, when you went on ahead to the floor, did you enlighten Gagern about his mistake? Did you say, 'Son, you've got it all wrong: the gal who's coming over here with Cartwright is not Tilly Parsons, but Monica Stanton from East Roystead? No, you didn't; and I'll prove it to you."

This time H.M. fastened his murderous glare on Howard Fisk, with such intensity that the director removed his arm from around the little blonde.

"Do you remember," pursued H.M., "the first words you said when you were introduced to Monica Stanton? *I* do, because they were all written down for me by W. Cartwright; but do you recall 'em?"

Mr. Fisk whistled.

He also seemed to be suffering the pangs of enlightenment.

"Good Lord, of course," he muttered, and gave Monica a ghostly smile. "I thought she was Tilly Parsons too. I said, *'Ah, the expert from Hollywood. Hackett mentioned it. I hope you won't find our English ways too slow for you.'* " He reflected. "And you're quite right. Hackett merely said to Gagern and me that the new writer was here, and was coming over to see us in charge of Bill Cartwright. We were too much upset about matters to discuss it."

H.M.'s cigar had gone out, but he did not relight it.

"And now, my fatheads," he continued, "I want to point out the one fact which (if you'd had your wits about you) would have let the cat out of the bag with a reverberatin' yowl.

"Unless a miracle had happened, you'd established that the mysterious pourer-of-the-acid must 'a' been one of five persons. It must have been either Frances Fleur, or Thomas Hackett, or Howard Fisk, or Bill Cartwright, or Kurt Gagern. Up to the time the acid was poured, our friend Gagern was the only one of five who hadn't met Monica Stanton. He was the only one who didn't know she was not Tilly Parsons. He was the only one who didn't know who she was and what she was. He was the only one who could have made a mistake. Naturally, he kept out of her way until after the pourin' of the acid; and when he came peepin' and pryin' in at that window afterward — burn me, what a shock *that* must have been!

"You can bet he kept out of 'Tilly Parsons's' way. All he got was a distant glimpse of her in a practically dark sound stage; and later, a peep at her head and shoulders from above when she walked into the doctor's house on an almost completely dark Eighteen-eight-two. Uh-huh. You." H.M. now pointed his cigar at Tilly. "What's the color of your hair?"

"You can do me a favor," said Tilly, "and call it golden."

"It's peroxided, ain't it?"

"Judas," muttered Tilly, "what a smooth, oily old flatterer *you* are. O.K., Ancient Mariner. It's peroxided."

"And how do you wear it?"

"Bobbed."

"Yes. Now take a long look at the Stanton gal; see the color of her hair, and how she wears it. I'd also like to know what kind of clothes you usually wear. I don't mean that sky-blue-pink piece of God-awfulness you got on at the moment," explained H.M., carefully defining his terms while Tilly turned purple, "I mean the kind of clothes you usually wear. Suits — hey? Gray or blue tailored suits? Uh-huh. And Monica Stanton was wearin' a gray tailored suit on the afternoon of August 23.

"Mind you, Joe Gagern was havin' some exceedingly bad luck. If he'd got so much as one good glance at the Stanton gal: if he'd seen her face by as much as the flicker of a match: he'd no more have mistaken her for you than he'd have mistaken a Michelangelo seraph for a desert buzzard by George Belcher. But he didn't get that glimpse. Even if he'd got a good chance to hear her voice, he still mightn't't'a' made it. But his only opportunity to hear her voice was through a metal speaking-tube, which would make Patti on her top note sound like Donald Duck in a thunderstorm; and so, d'ye see, the illusion was complete."

Tilly's eyes were glazed.

"I can't take it," she said. "The man's subtle flatteries are driving me nuts. If I can ever get over this attack of swelled head, I'll try to be nice to my friends afterward."

But this was bravado. Tilly suddenly shuddered, and there was a feeling of chill in the room.

Bill Cartwright did not notice this. Remembering Gagern peering into the window of the doctor's consulting-room afterward, his eyes glistening and turning on a line with the window ledge, Bill was filled with pardonable annoyance.

"And this annoyance," he declared, "I am going to get off my chest. You now tell me that all my theories about Gagern being guilty—which, you may recall, you reviled and ridiculed and spat upon—were true after all?"

"That's right, son."

"Then why in blazes couldn't you drop me a hint?"

H.M. was apologetic.

"Y'see, son, we might have been dealin' with very important matters. I couldn't tell. I had to make absolutely sure Joe wasn't tied up in an espionage plot. I didn't think he was. So far as bein' a possible spy was concerned, as I told Ken Blake, I could have sworn he was absolutely trustworthy. And so he was. There never was an espionage plot. But with regard to the other things—oh, my eye!—Joe's guilt was so obvious that it stuck out a mile. I had to give him rope and find out what his game really was.

"Joe thought it would be heartbreakin'ly easy to pull the wool over the old man's eyes. Note the dates. Middle of August: it's decided at Albion Films to import Tilly Parsons from America. Middle of August: Joe Gagern volunteers his services to me in case war breaks out. Reason? Ho ho! You guess it. Soon (very soon) his ex-wife will be thunderin' down on Pineham. He means to stop her from betrayin' his real identity. And he's got the colossal, stargazin' cheek to believe that, if he's suspected of bein' up to any funny business, he can always get *me* to protect him by announcing that he's one of my agents. He—"

H.M. paused, and glanced at Tilly.

241

"What name did he marry you under, by the way? They told me what it was when I talked to the Los Angeles police on the telephone Wednesday afternoon; but I sort of forget."

In spite of herself the tears stung into Tilly's eyes again.

"Fritz von Elbe," she snapped, blowing her nose violently on the handkerchief. "He wasn't a baron. He said he was a Major of Uhlans in the last war. You know: those guys with the funny hats."

"And?"

"And," snarled Tilly, "he forged one of my cheques for fifteen thousand dollars, and pulled his freight. That was how he was able to . . . never mind." She put away the handkerchief. "I told Bill Cartwright once how much I hated fakes, and what a fake *he* was!"

H.M. nodded.

"It also being very rummy and very significant," he pursued, "that two days before Tilly Parsons (the real one this time) arrives at Pineham, Gagern falls into the lake and is laid up with the 'flu. He himself, d'ye see, frankly admitted to me that he'd never met her face to face. But that's getting ahead of the story. At the time of the acid-pouring affair—"

"What about his alibi for that time?" demanded Bill.

"You mean," said H.M., with what in anybody else would have been a fiendish grin, "when he was supposed to be talkin' to me on the telephone?"

"Yes?"

"His alibi," said H.M., "was eyewash. The feller's a fatheaded fool, compounded in equal parts of delusion and conceit. All he did was ring up and tell me firmly he was talking at ten minutes past five. Lord love a duck! Any bloke who's got the bewilderin' cheek to try that trick on a man with an office in easy sound of Big Ben, is asking for even more trouble than I hope he gets.

"Actually, he spoke to me just before five. But I thought it would be very salutary, very fine and soothin' to the soul," murmured H.M., settling back into his chair, "if I just backed him up and waited to see what happened.

"Then he thought he was all prepared. He wrote his message on the blackboard, 'Tell the lady who came in with Mr. Cartwright—' "

"In my handwriting," growled Tilly.

"In your handwriting. That's right. Joe Collins Gagern thought that was a stroke of sheer genius. He was goin' to blind you with acid, and the message should be in *your* handwriting.

"And then what? Ah! From a long distance off, dim and misty out of the edge of the light, what does he see? He sees (he thinks) his two wives sittin' in campchairs and having a little chat together as cosily as you please."

"You mean," cried Monica, "he saw me with Miss Fleur?"

"He saw your back, that's all. I seem distinctly to remember your statement saying that Frances Fleur 'looked over your shoulder,' and then all of a sudden got up and excused herself."

Bill Cartwright, at this point, did not get up and excuse himself. But he did get up and execute a dance of hatred and anguish.

"By the ten thousand whistling devils of nearer Andalusia!" raved Bill. "By Abaddon. Lord of the Bottomless Pit! By . . . so I was even right about that too? He beckoned to F.F., and called her away on some tomfool errand, so that he could get his 'other wife' alone?"

"Ask her, son," said H.M.

Miss Fleur did not seem to be so much affected by this whole recital as Tilly. But now and then there was a lurking fear about her fine eyes.

"Men," she complained, "are so *queer.*"

"Oh, my God!" moaned Tilly.

"But they are, you know. There was my first husband. Poor Ronnie," said Miss Fleur. "Going about making faces at servant-girls, and all that. I daresay it's all right if it's kept to your own home. But when it comes to going and making faces at other people's servants through the windows — well, really. I mean to say."

Tilly regarded her with awe.

"Lady," Tilly said, "there's one thing you can't complain about, anyway. You sure do get variety in your marriages. If you can only land a strangler or a pyromaniac for your third venture, you'll be in clover. Besides — "

"That's right," Miss Fleur said thoughtfully. "I'm not really married at all, am I?"

"No, you're not," said Tilly, not without spite. "You're a betrayed woman, that's what you are. You've been living in sin. Foo!"

Miss Fleur considered this.

"I haven't," she declared. "But poor Kurt has." She hesitated. "Do you know, I thought there was something queer about it, when he called me over from

244

Monica and said I must go and study the *Brünhilde*
smoking-room set straightaway, or I wouldn't have the
business right. I came back for a minute, and saw him
slipping a bottle inside the door of one of the dummy
houses on Eighteen-eighty-two. When he walked away
I picked up the bottle, and it sizzled. I didn't know
what it was; I still don't; but I thought it was all right
because Kurt said it was. So I put the bottle back
before he should come and catch me."

Again she hesitated.

"After all, don't be too hard on him. He deceived me
dreadfully, but he must have been terribly fond of me
to do all that, mustn't he?"

"You may put it at that," observed Howard Fisk,
mildly. "It was probably the one genuine emotion that
chap has ever had. But with all due respect to your . . .
er . . . shattered heart, Frances, let Sir Henry go on.
Gagern made his first attempt, with the acid. He
failed. But he saw—"

"He saw," replied H.M., "with the clear, dazzling
light of inspiration, that he'd been handed a boon on a
platter."

"Everybody at Pineham was now firmly convinced
that somebody was trying to kill Monica Stanton.
Admirable! Let 'em go on thinkin' so. For Joe Gagern
looked at himself in the mirror, and he turned dizzy.
He realized how much his new life meant to him, and
his new wife, and his new position. He couldn't, physically *couldn't,* let Tilly Parsons come in and blow that
to glory. There was only one thing to do. He went from
fraud to vitriol-throwing, and . . ."

"And so to murder," said Bill.

"And so to murder, yes. But he'd been granted a

beautiful opportunity. If he just up and killed Tilly Parsons straight out, it might be awkward. Very awkward. If somebody began lookin' too closely into motives for killin' her, the past might get up out of its grave and dance the Big Apple all over him. But—suppose Tilly Parsons died, and everybody thought the blow had been aimed at Monica Stanton?"

"Pure safety."

"Everybody would say what a sad mistake it was, and go harin' off after motives for attacking the Stanton gal. And he would be serene.

"So he underlined the menace to Monica Stanton. Burn me, how he underlined it! He wrote those anonymous letters. He went yellin' outside the windows with a very passable imitation of Tilly's voice, and fired that shot through the window, on the night Bill Cartwright very nearly caught him.

"Of course that shot was never intended to hit you." He looked at Monica. "It was never intended to come anywhere near you. On the contrary, if his aim was the slightest bit woozy and he did happen to kill you, his scheme was dished for good and all. And he very nearly did hit you, because Cartwright—in yankin' you back from the window—dragged you straight into the path of the bullet."

"So I'm the villain of the piece again, am I?" inquired Bill, not without bitterness.

"You were in Gagern's eyes, son," H.M. assured him somberly. "For three weeks you'd been on his tail. For three weeks you'd made it almost impossible for him to act. And something had to be done about it.

"So Gagern, now ready for real business, played his ace of trumps.

"He thought he'd persuade me *(me)* to get you into my office and beg you with tears in my eyes to let him alone. Ho ho! Do you think for one minute, if I hadn't known he was a wrong 'un, I'd have betrayed to any outsider in this cosmos the name of any of my men?" H.M. shook his head with broad and fishy skepticism. "Not so you could notice it, son. If my fellers aren't good enough to dodge their difficulties without a signed testimonial from me, they're no good to me or anybody else.

"So he sat in my office, and he told us that little pack of ghost stories. Every word of it rang false as a lead shilling, if you noticed. He was just a little *too* grand. He was just a little *too* actor-y.

"He completed his game by throwin' a dash of suspicion at Tilly Parsons herself. Not too much, mind you. He wouldn't swear, in so many words, that the woman at Pineham wasn't Tilly Parsons: those things can be checked up on. He admitted having been in Hollywood, in case the fact ever came out. But it would be a fine stroke if he could incriminate Tilly Parsons as bein' concerned in the menace to Monica Stanton . . . and then Tilly Parsons, either a suicide or the victim of a mistake, drops over dead.

"At the end of that interview in my office, I had the breeze up badly. It was plain as print that the real business was now about to happen. And it happened even sooner than I thought it would, for a very good reason. What I couldn't guess, then, was *how* it might happen."

H.M. leaned forward.

"You know now how he worked that trick with the poisoned cigarette, don't you?" he asked.

There was more than a slight uproar, quelled by Thomas Hackett.

"No, I'm hanged if I do," Mr. Hackett protested. "Gagern (rot him) was the only one of us who couldn't have done it. He was the only one of us who couldn't possibly have slipped the poisoned cigarette into the box."

"But d'ye see, son," said H.M. patiently, "there never was any poisoned cigarette in the box."

"What?"

"I said, son, there never was any poisoned cigarette in the box."

"But—"

"Well, work it out for yourselves," said H.M. "You," he looked at Monica, "Bought fifty cigarettes and put 'em into an empty box. Nobody smoked any of those cigarettes until *you,*" here he glared at Tilly, "took one at about seven-thirty. Right?"

"Yes."

"Yes: but if somebody had slipped a poisoned cigarette in there, there would have been fifty-one in the box. Wouldn't there? So when you took a cigarette away from the store, that should have left fifty. Shouldn't it? Yes. But when we counted 'em there were only forty-nine. Which means, my good fathead, that what you took out of the box was a perfectly harmless, ordinary Player's cigarette; and that somebody deftly exchanged it for a poisoned one after you walked back into your office."

"Boloney!" shrilled Tilly.

She was in wild earnest about this. She held up her hand.

"Listen, Ancient Mariner," she said. "I'll string along with you on the other things, but not there. Judas, I'm the victim! I ought to know, oughtn't I? And the cigarette with the dope in it was the same cigarette I got out of the box in the other room."

"No, it wasn't, my wench."

"But I was *smoking* the blooming thing! Can you tell me it could have been changed on me when I was smoking it?"

"Sure."

"Well?"

H.M. sniffed. He regarded his fingers disconsolately. Then he eyed Tilly.

"You drink a lot of coffee, don't you?"

"That's right."

"Keep the kettle boilin' all day? Forget about it and never notice until it starts to shoot out geysers of steam?"

"Yes."

"And what do you do when you notice the place gettin' full of steam?"

"Why," said Tilly, "I go into the cloak-room and turn it off. I put down my cigarette on the edge of the standing ashtray, and walk into the cloak-room, and . . ." Tilly stopped Her eyes widened, and grew fixed. "Sweet, suffering Moses!" she whispered.

H.M. nodded.

"Leaving the cigarette on the edge of the ashtray," he agreed. "I knew you did by all the burns on the edge of it; and people here tell me they've often seen you do it.

"Whereupon crafty Joe Gagern, who's already pinched most of your Chesterfields when you walked out to the front door with Hackett and Fisk, simply walks in by the corridor door. In his hand he's got another lighted cigarette. That's the whole trick — that one *lighted* cigarette looks exactly like another.

"He switches the cigarettes and walks out again. They can't see him in the communicating room because the door (as usual) is closed. You can't hear him because the floor is brick covered with linoleum. You came back; and, seein' a lighted cigarette, naturally think it's the one you put down. The beauty of that scheme bein' that the very victim herself thinks it's a cigarette she got from the other room."

Tilly seemed hypnotized.

Again she made a gesture of protest.

"But all that," she insisted, "depends on getting me out of the office and into the cloak-room? Doesn't it?"

"Sure."

"It depends upon the kettle boiling over?" demanded Tilly. "But how could he know the kettle would boil over just as soon as I came back with my cigarette?"

"Because," returned H.M., "all he had to do was reach through the service-hatch and turn up the gas."

H.M. glared at them.

"I hope you people haven't forgotten that, in the wall of the cloak-room, just over the gas-ring and communicating with the corridor outside, there's an old service-hatch." He peered at Monica, who did remember it very vividly. "Don't under any circumstances forget it. It's the key to Joe Gagern's scheme. It was his observation post and his listening post. From that hatch-window he could hear every word his victim said and follow every move she made."

There was a silence, after which Bill Cartwright swore with such comprehensiveness that Monica shushed him.

"Of course," pursued H.M. drowsily, "Joe had been plannin' it for days or even weeks. He'd been goin' about with that cigarette in his pocket, waiting for the proper time.

"On Wednesday afternoon, Joe and Bill Cartwright left my office at half-past four—we've established that. We've later been able to check up on his movements. He excused himself to Cartwright, saying he was goin' to meet his wife. He didn't; he left a message for her at the Excelsior Club, and came straight out here.

"He hadn't necessarily established that he was goin' to act that night. He was goin' to hang about and see whether the right opportunity might not bob up. And then he had to act. Why? Because, lurking as usual, he discovered that Tilly was winding up her last sequence and was going back to America. Whereupon Joe Collins Gagern von Elbe made his last, worst bloomer. He couldn't let her go, and shudder back into safety again. He'd become just a little loony on the subject of the woman who was ruining his peace of mind. So the fool had to go and do it. He let the trap spring, he switched the cigarettes, and he walked straight into my lovin' arms."

Again there was a silence. Mr. Hackett automatically handed round fresh drinks; and the spirits of the company, damped for a time, began to rise again. Tilly

Parsons chuckled. She surveyed H.M. with real interest.

"You know," she observed, "you are a crafty old son of a so-and-so, Ancient Mariner."

"I'm the old man," said H.M., drawing himself up with dignity. "And anybody who tries to pull the wool over my eyes because he thinks I'm shakin' and dodderin' my way down into the House of Lords . . . cor! I could chew nails every time I think of it. Still, I expect," he peered at them over his spectacles, "I expect you're all feeling a little bit better, aren't you?"

"Ever so much better," said Monica, fervently and happily.

"What about you, son?"

For answer Bill again set Monica on his lap, squared his shoulders, accepted a drink, and prepared to talk. For fully an hour he had been obliged to keep more or less silent, and he was now ready to give his eloquence a really satisfactory gallop.

"Relief," he said, "I confess to be the second most dominant feeling in my life at the current time. The first and most dominant feeling I need not mention, since it will be obvious to all right-minded people. At the same time, sir, I confess that as yet I am far from thoroughly satisfied—"

"Bill!"

"Light of my life," he said, putting his finger on her ear and tracing the line of it, "you have got the wires crossed. That too I admit; but, curiously enough, I was not referring to it. I mean that at least one point in the evidence has not been satisfactorily cleared up. What in blazes happened to that film?"

"Eh, son?"

"The missing film. The exterior shots that have been causing half the row here. Where are they? Who took them? Did Gagern do it, to lend color to his story? Or what happened?"

Mr. Hackett drew himself up.

"The matter," he said rather grandly, "has been satisfactorily adjusted. We have them back, I am glad to say."

"Yes, I gathered that. But where were they? What happened to them? Doesn't anybody know?"

"Efficiency," said Mr. Hackett, "by which I mean real, true efficiency, has always been the watchword of Albion films. That's what I told Mr. Marshlake; and it will, I know—"

"Tom, come off it. *What happened to that film?*"

Mr. Hackett told him.

4

And so the shortening evening drew in across Pineham asleep, and a wind rustled among yellowing trees, and a brilliant moon rose over the sound-stages.

Monica Stanton and Bill Cartwright, at a restaurant in town, were deciding that in these days there was no reason why Cornwall shouldn't do just as well as Capri for a honeymoon. Frances Fleur was at another party, drinking orange juice and talking to a Scandinavian tenor whose top notes could break a window at twenty yards. Thomas Hackett was happily in the cutting-room. Howard Fisk was explaining the finer points of acting to his new find. Tilly Parsons was packing her bags at the Merefield County Club; and, it is to be feared, crying a little.

But, though quiet, Pineham was not altogether silent. As the great moon rose in majesty above the sound stages, its benevolent rays illuminated the heads of two men who were standing in the main drive.

One was a short fat man with a cigar, the other a tall spectacled young man with an ultra-refined accent.

"Lookit," said the fat man. "It's a knockout! It's stupendous! It's gigantic! It's colossal! Jeez, it'll knock every box-office for a loop from here to South Bend, Indiana."

"I am gratified to hear you say so, Mr. Aaronson."

"Boy," said the fat man, "you ain't heard the half of it. Lookit. Did you see the final rushes yesterday?"

"No, Mr. Aaronson."

"Lookit. It's the end of the Battle of Waterloo, see?"

"Yes, Mr. Aaronson."

"And the Duke of Wellington is lying wounded on his camp-bed, see? And Sam McFiggis, see, he writes us a swell poem to go with it. It starts, 'For I slipped into the future, far as human eyes could see—' "

"Dipped, Mr. Aaronson."

"What do you mean, dipped?"

"Dipped, Mr. Aaronson, not slipped. I fear Mr. McFiggis is not the author of the lines. They are from Tennyson's *Locksley Hall*. The text runs:

> *"For I dipped into the future, far as human eye*
> *could see,*
> *Saw the vision of the world, and all the wonder*
> *that*
> *would be,*

"Ok., O.K., if you say so. But lookit. Here's the Duke of Wellington, see? Close-up, and slow fade-out. I thought that was the end of the rushes. Only it wasn't. It fades in a big picture of Portsmouth navy yard."

"Of what, Mr. Aaronson?"

"Ain't I telling you? Of Portsmouth navy yard. Then a close-up of Winston Churchill, with a derby hat on, smoking a cigar. Everybody in the projection-room, see, starts to cheer and applaud and holler—"

"But Mr. Aaronson—"

"I'm telling you. Then some of the swellest action shots you ever saw. Battleships in action; close-ups of guns; planes diving; boats laying mines across some funny-looking harbor. Boy, was it a honey, or wasn't it?"

"But, Mr. Aaronson—"

"Well, when we'd been watching it about ten minutes, I leans over to Oakeshott Harrison and says, 'Lookit, I said, 'it's swell. It's stupendous! It's colossal! But there's too much of it. Can't you cut it down a little bit? And he says, 'Mr. Aaronson, I will not tell you a lie, *I* didn't shoot them scenes.' I said, 'You didn't?' He says, 'Mr. Aaronson, to be perfectly frank with you, I don't know what they're doing in the picture at all.'—Can you imagine that?"

"Yes, Mr. Aaronson."

"And then, see, in the middle of it, in comes Tom Hackett of Albion Films. And he starts to jump up and down and holler, 'You stole my exteriors; you stole my exteriors.'"

"And had you, Mr. Aaronson?"

"Jeez, no! But lookit. I'll be a son of a gun if they didn't turn out to be his after all. Can you tie that?"

"Yes, Mr. Aaronson."

"You think maybe there must have been maybe a mistake somewhere?"

"I consider it extremely probable, Mr. Aaronson."

"Well, it's all right. Because it gives us the idea, see? We'll get our own shots, and we'll put 'em straight in the picture, see; and, boy, will it be a honey or won't it? But lookit. I don't get this. How do you suppose the shots got into our picture, anyway?"

"I dare not venture a guess, Mr. Aaronson. I should say that it was just one of those things that happen in the film business."

The fat man drew a deep and happy sigh. Radiant was the moonlight; radiant was the future; radiant was the world.

"Boy," he said, "you sure said it. You sure got something there. It's just one of those things that happen in the film business."

THE END